LEGION
BOOK
TWO

FIRE
& EARTH

A.D. STARRLING

DEDICATION

To my father

1942-2019

COPYRIGHT

Fire and Earth (Legion Book Two)

Edited by Right Ink On The Wall
Cover design by 17 Studio Book Design

Want to know about AD Starrling's upcoming releases? Sign up to her
newsletter for new release alerts, sneak peeks, giveaways, and more.

www.ADStarrling.com

PROLOGUE

YASHIRO KURODA STEPPED OUT OF THE BLACK SEDAN and paused to look at the sky to the west. The setting sun was an orange fireball dipping below the dark line of the Pacific Ocean, way out beyond the surf crashing onto Long Beach. Above it, the heavens were scored with a dizzying kaleidoscope of ever-changing reds and purples.

A trace of disquiet danced at the edge of his consciousness as he gazed upon the crimson hues tainting the horizon.

"Is everything okay, sir?" one of his bodyguards murmured.

Yashiro hesitated before dipping his chin at the hard-faced man beside him. "Yes, thank you, Riuji. I was thinking of a silly superstition. One Haruki and I learned of when we were still living in Kyushu." He grimaced. "Among the many other garish stories told to us by our nannies."

Riuji Ogawa studied the blood-red sky. "It is a rather ominous color."

Kaito Sasaki climbed out of the vehicle behind them

and stood nervously watching the dark building they had pulled up in front of, his briefcase clasped to his chest. For once, Yashiro couldn't blame the skittish man. Tian Gao Lee, the Triad gang leader they had come to discuss business with, had chosen a rather unsavory spot for their meeting.

Yashiro headed for the main door of the run-down warehouse with Riuji, Sasaki, and Masato, his second bodyguard.

"Master Haruki will be back the day after tomorrow, won't he?" Riuji murmured as they crossed the blacktop.

"Yes." Yashiro sighed. "Though why he had to go all the way to Stanford to get his MBA is beyond me. At least he'll be home for his birthday."

Riuji maintained a diplomatic silence.

They both knew the reason why Yashiro's younger brother had chosen a university so far away to get his business degree.

They slowed when they entered the shadow of the building. Yashiro scanned the empty parking lot at the side with a faint frown.

"Their cars must be out back," Riuji said, his tone cautious.

Yashiro smiled faintly, grateful once more for the man's presence. Riuji had been in the employ of the Kuroda Group for twenty-five years and his personal bodyguard for almost as long. The man had always been able to read him, even when Yashiro was still a snot-nosed, little brat.

Darkness and silence greeted them when they stepped inside the warehouse. Yashiro's eyes slowly adapted to the gloom. Shapes materialized out of the shadows.

A sudden wave of tension emanated from Riuji and Masato. Yashiro stiffened, his senses on high alert.

Fifty feet away, beyond the carcasses of abandoned machinery and piles of rusting drums, a group of people stood silently watching them from the other end of the abandoned depot.

"Is that you, Tian Gao?" Yashiro called out in a steady voice. He could hear Sasaki breathing fast next to him.

For a moment, there was no reply. A cigarette lighter suddenly flicked into life, the click so loud it echoed around the vast space.

Sasaki gasped and startled in the shadows to his right. Yashiro ignored the man and watched the dancing, yellow flame illuminate a scarred and ghoulish face across the way.

"Who else were you expecting, Kuroda?" Tian Gao Lee said gruffly.

A spotlight came on and washed across the interior of the building.

Yashiro relaxed as he gazed upon the familiar, pock-marked features of the Triad gang leader. He ignored the inner voice warning him that something was off and closed the distance to Tian Gao and his entourage.

There was no way the man would jeopardize the alliance between the Triad and the Kuroda Group. Not after the years of gang warfare and bloodshed that had preceded their current truce.

Riuji's expression remained guarded, he and the other bodyguard sticking close to Yashiro.

Yashiro stopped a few feet from Tian Gao and examined the other man with a neutral smile. "Of all the places you could have chosen for our meeting, this does not exactly suit your flamboyant style."

The corner of Tian Gao's mouth hitched in a lopsided smirk. "You mean it doesn't suit yours, don't you?"

Yashiro sighed. "There is nothing wrong with liking the finer things in life, Tian Gao." He scanned the faces of the silent men behind the Triad gang leader. "I see you've had a change of personnel. Did you get bored with your old guard?"

Something flashed across Tian Gao's face for a second.

He shrugged. "I decided to make some new friends."

Yashiro stared. It was a strange term for the Triad gang leader to use in relation to the men in his employ. His gaze moved to the watchful figures behind Tian Gao once more. Though he couldn't quite put a finger on the why, there was something about them that was putting his nerves on edge.

"How's your old man keeping?" Tian Gao said.

"My father is fine, thank you," Yashiro murmured. "And how's your boss?"

Tian Gao grimaced. "As tight-assed as ever."

Yashiro started to smile. That was when it came to him. The reason why the men with Tian Gao were making him uneasy.

They're not blinking.

Fear washed over Yashiro then. An irrational, gut-wrenching fear that stemmed from the most primitive part of his brain. With it came a sudden premonition.

We'll be lucky if we get out of here alive.

Riuji glanced at him, the stiff set of his shoulders telling Yashiro he had also picked up on the strange vibe coming from the men with Tian Gao. Yashiro avoided the bodyguard's gaze and kept his eyes firmly on the Triad gang leader.

"Now that we've exchanged pleasantries, let's talk business, shall we?" he said in a light voice.

Tian Gao's expression grew sober. "Yes, let's."

He walked up to Yashiro and punched his right fist straight through his chest.

Yashiro gasped and rocked back on his heels, fingers rising instinctively to grip the other man's wrist. Shock reverberated through him as he looked down to where Tian Gao's hand had disappeared inside his body.

Impossible! That's impossi—

The pain came with a fury that robbed him of his breath. Yashiro grunted and sagged to his knees. Screams reached him, the sounds echoing dimly above the loud roar of blood in his ears. He turned his head stiffly and saw the men with Tian Gao tear Riuji and Masato from limb to limb.

Except they weren't men. Not anymore.

As the horror of what was unfolding before him finally registered in his mind and coldness swamped his body, Yashiro realized that the gruesome folk tales of his child-hood were not made-up stories after all. That monsters did exist and that they walked this world inside the bodies of ordinary-looking men.

"Why?" Yashiro whispered.

Something hot bubbled up his throat and filled his mouth with a coppery taste. Blood burst from his lips. It splattered onto the clothes of the man who had his fingers wrapped around his heart.

Yashiro stared up at Tian Gao. The thing that looked back at him smiled savagely, features distorted by the beast within.

"Don't take this personally, Kuroda," Tian Gao said, his words underscored by a faint animal growl. "This is just business."

Yashiro's gaze found the remains of his bodyguards. The creatures who had killed the two men were crouched over them, hands and mouths filled with gore as they feasted upon the flesh of their victims.

Rage erupted inside Yashiro. He gritted his teeth, his racing pulse throbbing through his body with every beat of his dying heart as he called upon the last reserves of his strength and courage.

This is unbecoming of me. I am the heir to the Kuroda Group, goddammit!

He lowered his right hand from Tian Gao's arm, flicked his wrist, and sliced through the Triad gang leader's forearm with the spring-loaded blade that appeared from beneath the cuff of his suit.

Tian Gao roared and staggered back a couple of steps, his severed limb spraying out a black liquid that splashed onto the ground and stained his clothes.

Yashiro reached for the stump still embedded inside his body and ripped it out of his chest with a guttural cry.

Sound faded. The world shrank to a rapidly diminishing circle of darkness.

Yashiro thudded onto his side. The last thing he saw before death claimed him in an icy embrace was his bloody, battered heart shuddering to a stop inside Tian Gao's hand on the ground before him.

CHAPTER ONE

ARTEMUS STEELE FISTED HIS HANDS AT HIS SIDES AND stared at the woman before him. She sat at a table with a cracked, red, linoleum top in the middle of a squalid kitchen in a run-down apartment above a laundromat in Kansas City.

Shelley Steele was but a ghost of the woman Artemus had left twelve years ago, the day he ran away from the second home he had ever known. Gaunt, her skin sallow and loose, her hollow-cheeked features sagging as if she hadn't eaten a decent meal in days, Artemus's mother looked like she had aged several decades since the last time he'd seen her.

"Tell me," Artemus repeated, his tone cold despite the heat that flooded his chest and made it hard for him to breathe. "I want you to look me in the eye and tell me that I'm really your son."

His mother flinched, her fingers whitening around the cooling coffee cup she grasped like a lifeline. She raised her chin and met his gaze head-on.

"You are my son," she said in a low voice.

Pain stabbed through Artemus. "You're lying."

Although over two decades had passed since that day, Artemus still blamed himself for what had happened to his family following the incident that had occurred on the night of his sixth birthday. An incident the ramifications of which were not to manifest themselves for another twenty-two years.

After his father had lost his job and turned to drinking so heavily he passed his days in a near catatonic state, Artemus's mother had finally garnered the courage to leave him and their abusive marriage. Artemus had come home from school one day when he was in second grade to find her standing on the drive with two suitcases and bus tickets to Kansas City. They'd stayed with his mother's sister for a few weeks before renting a cheap apartment a short walk from where his mother had found a waitressing job. Though they had been dirt poor and Artemus had been bullied at school for his thrift shop clothes and shoes, they'd been happy for a while.

He'd been eight when she'd brought home her first boyfriend. That was when Artemus had realized something he'd never known about her. She needed a man in her life to feel secure. It didn't matter if the guy was a cheating, lying bastard who liked to use her as a punching bag. Or that the ones who came afterward started using Artemus as the object upon which to vent their anger and frustration at how small and insignificant their lives were.

The day Artemus showed his mother the bruises from his first beating when he was eleven, she turned around and told him he must have done something to deserve it. In that moment, he'd stared at her and realized he was looking at a stranger. The woman who'd read him bedtime stories when he was a child and who'd snuggled up with him on the sofa on rainy Sunday afternoons to watch old black and white movies on TV was no more. She'd become someone else, someone pallid and weak, someone who seemed happy to listen to the lies of her lovers rather than believe her own child and acknowledge the brutality that had been visited upon him. It had taken Artemus another couple of years to find his resolve to leave her and three more to plan his escape.

"If you are truly my mother, then tell me about him," Artemus said bitterly.

She blinked at him then, a confused frown wrinkling her brow. "About who?"

Artemus took a step toward the table and leaned his hands on the cracked surface, conscious he was looming over her and not really giving a damn. "Tell me about my brother."

His mother drew a sharp breath. Shock flared across her face.

"What—what do you mean?!"

"I have a brother," Artemus said. "A twin. His name is Drake. Drake Hunter."

The color drained from his mother's face.

"That's impossible!" she blurted out. "I never gave birth to—"

She stopped abruptly and bit her lower lip.

Ah. We finally get to the crux of the matter.

Although Artemus didn't want to hear the answers the woman in front of him was holding on to, didn't want to learn that his whole childhood had been based on lies, he knew he had no option but to uncover the truth. His life depended on it, as did the lives of the companions he had gained three weeks ago, when Fate had decided to throw him a curve ball and his destiny had become linked to the people he now called his friends.

"Drake is my brother. I know this for certain," Artemus said in a low voice. "I've probably known it since the day I first met him, somewhere deep inside." He stared coldly at the woman opposite him. "Which means you either abandoned him when we were still infants, or you're not our mother."

She gazed at him, ashen-faced. "I—I don't—"

She lapsed into silence, her throat working convulsively.

A car horn sounded outside. Sirens blared in the distance. Artemus waited.

A shudder finally shook his mother. She closed her eyes, as if she couldn't bear to look at him.

"I was at my parents' farm when I gave birth," she started in a small, faltering voice. "Gary forced me to go home for my confinement. He didn't want to be there for the delivery and he said a newborn would only interfere with his work." She paused and swallowed, tears shimmering on her eyelashes. "The baby was stillborn. I didn't want to believe it at first. So I dressed him and wrapped him in a blanket and tried to nurse him. My parents let me be. They knew it was my way of grieving." She looked up at Artemus. "It was your cry that woke me the next night. The cry of a hungry baby. For a moment, I thought it was my own dead child come back to life, by some sort of miracle. But I looked at his cold, blue face where he lay next to me in my bed and knew this to be a lie."

Her voice broke. She wiped the tears streaming down her face and took a labored breath. "We found you in the field next to the barn. You were naked and wrapped in a plain, woolen blanket. It was my father who spotted you."

A tremulous smile curved her lips. "Your hair was so fair, it practically glowed in the moonlight. When I gazed upon your face and held you in my arms, it felt like Fate had guided me to you. That you were meant to be mine."

Artemus's vision blurred as he watched the crying woman seated at the table. His chest was so tight he felt it would burst at any moment. Love, hate, bitterness, gratitude, regret. They all filled his heart in a violent torrent of conflicting emotions.

"I was alone? When you found me?" he said at last.

His mother nodded shakily. "Yes."

"And you never tried to—" Artemus paused and ran a hand down his face, his fingers trembling. "You never tried to find out who I really was?"

"I did," his mother said quietly.

Artemus startled, shocked by her unexpected reply.

His mother's eyes filled with sorrow and remorse as she looked at him. "I checked the papers and made calls to the local hospital and the sheriff's office to ask if anyone had reported a missing child. No one had."

Silence filled the space between them as Artemus digested what she had just told him. He opened his mouth, hesitated, and clenched his jaw.

There was nothing left to say.

Artemus twisted on his heels and headed wordlessly for the front door of the dingy apartment. He paused on the threshold, aware that she had risen from the table and followed him into the hallway. He took a shallow breath and willed his painful, racing heart to slow down.

"Thank you," he said quietly, his back to her. "Thank you for being my mom for all those years. I was...happy. For a lot of it."

He left the apartment and headed briskly down the

gloomy, narrow stairwell, Shelley Steele's sobs fading in the distance behind him.

Sunlight dazzled Artemus when he stepped outside the building. He raised his face to the pale blue sky and inhaled deeply, letting the cold air fill his lungs. The reality of what had just happened sank in all over again.

He was an orphan. Had always been one. Like Drake. Except *he* had been given a chance at a family life, while his brother had been abandoned in the care of the state. And Artemus had also had Karl and Elton LeBlanc after he got to Chicago. Though they were not related by blood, Artemus had considered the two men more his family than his own father and mother.

A wave of unexpected anger rushed through him as he thought of his and Drake's real parents, whoever and wherever the hell they were.

I won't forgive them for deserting us.

An icy wind cooled his hot cheeks and sent a shiver dancing through him. Though winter was drawing to an end, it was still chilly out. He tucked his hands inside the pockets of his windbreaker and headed briskly up the sidewalk to a parked, black BMW superbike. A man with dark hair and eyes was leaning back against it, arms and ankles crossed.

"So, was it as you suspected?" Drake Hunter said quietly when Artemus stopped beside him.

Artemus nodded wordlessly. It was he who'd suggested that Drake come with him on this trip. If there had been answers to be found here today, then his brother deserved to be in on it.

Something that looked like sympathy flashed in the other man's hooded gaze. "We'd better head off if we want to make it back by nightfall."

He slipped his tinted visor on his face, tossed an identical one at Artemus, and climbed on the bike.

Artemus frowned as he caught the smart glasses. "I thought you said I could ride that thing back to Chicago."

"Did I?"

Drake tapped the throttle and made the engine growl. "You did."

A haughty smile curved Drake's lips. "Well, if I did, it was probably to shut you up. Now, get on before I decide to leave your sorry ass on this sidewalk."

Artemus scowled, put the visor on, and straddled the back of the bike.

Drake stiffened. "Hey, Goldilocks."

Artemus sighed at the nickname he'd inherited a few weeks ago. "What?"

"That had better be your gun digging in my buttcheek."

"Don't flatter yourself, asshole."

CHAPTER TWO

RAIN FELL FROM THE OVERCAST SKY IN THICK SHEETS that painted the world gray. It pummeled the ground and everything beneath it with savage intensity, raising a fine, white mist that clouded the air, and churning the exposed earth to mud.

Haruki Kuroda stared at the stone grave before him, raindrops mixing with the tears coursing freely down his face. He did not sob. He did not wail. He did not make so much as a sound. To do so would be to dishonor the memory of his brother. Instead, he gripped the prayer beads Yashiro had intended to give him that very day so hard his fingers bled.

Motion to the right drew Haruki's gaze. He looked at his father as the latter turned without so much as a backward glance and headed along the stone path that would take him to his town car, his escort following in his steps.

Today was Haruki's twenty-fifth birthday. It was also the day that would now forever be known as the one when the Kuroda Group buried its legitimate heir. And Akihito Kuroda, the head of the Kuroda Group, had treated both his eldest son's funeral and his youngest son's birthday with the same glacial demeanor with which he did everything else in life.

As the shateigashira of Ishida Kanzaki, their kumichō and the head of the syndicate their organization fell under, he could not be seen to be sentimental. Especially not when the authority of the Kuroda Group had been so shockingly called into question by Yashiro's murder.

Haruki knew all of this. He knew it, yet he could not stop the burning resentment that filled his soul at his father's blatant lack of emotion. He'd thought that of the two of them, his father would have shown some sign of grief at Yashiro's untimely death.

I know I don't deserve our father's affection. I am the bastard child, after all. But Yashiro? Yashiro deserved tears at least.

Pain twisted Haruki's heart as he gazed upon his brother's final resting place once more.

Yashiro's mother had died when the boy was three years old. Two years after his wife's passing, Akihito Kuroda's mistress had given birth to Haruki. When she too perished five years later, Haruki was forcibly taken from his maternal grandparents and brought into the Kuroda Group to be raised as Yashiro's half-brother and the second heir to the organization.

But members of the Kuroda Group refused to accept that the illegitimate child of a lowly office worker could one day rule over them. And so Haruki's new life in the Kuroda household became a living hell. Shunned and mocked by the ones he had been bound to against his will, he did the only thing he could. He rebelled. It wasn't long before he earned himself a reputation in the underworld he inhabited. The reputation of a young savage. Of a hotblooded animal who would as soon punch your lights out as look at you.

That got him expelled from school so often his father eventually decided to have him tutored at home. And it was in his books that Haruki had discovered his ticket out of the Kuroda Group.

The only light in the darkness that had been Haruki's daily existence at the time had been Yashiro. His older brother had been the one person who had ever treated Haruki with decency and respect. And love. There had been a genuine bond between them from the very start, when they were growing up in Kyushu. One forged as much by their shared Fate as it was by blood.

Yashiro had always had his back, especially when it came to dealing with their father.

That morning, their housekeeper had given Haruki the birthday gift his brother had purchased for him on a recent trip to Hong Kong. Lying inside the beautiful, carved, red ebony box he had unwrapped had been an onyx juzu bracelet, the principal bead taking the form of a metal dragon head with ruby eyes. Haruki's vision had blurred with unshed tears when he'd gazed upon it. He could tell the bracelet was of the highest quality. It had probably cost Yashiro an arm and a leg.

Haruki looked down at the gift his brother had given him. He lifted it slowly to the rain and watched the heavy drops wash away the blood coating the precious beads. The tumultuous thoughts and feelings that had swirled inside him like a tempest since he learned of Yashiro's murder crystalized into a cold conviction.

Though he'd thought he could finally escape the cold-hearted world he had been born into, Haruki realized there would be no way out for him now. Whether he liked it or not, the mantle of being the heir to the Kuroda Group would now be his burden to bear. That was, if the head of their syndicate gave his approval. If Ishida Kanzaki officially recognized him as the Kuroda Group's successor, Haruki knew he would have to assume the title fully if he wished to attain his goals.

"I swear an oath to you, brother." He slipped the cleansed bracelet onto his right wrist. "I swear I will find the one who killed you. And I will not rest until I bring you his head. Even if it costs me my life, I *will* avenge you."

Haruki twisted on his heels and headed down the path his father had taken, heedless of the rain soaking him to the bone and the somber escort at his back.

IT WASN'T UNTIL DINNER LATER THAT EVENING THAT Haruki's father finally said his first words of the day to him.

"I hope now that you are twenty-five, you will start to act your age," Akihito Kuroda said coldly from where he sat at the head of the table.

Haruki paused, his fingers clenching slightly on the stem of the wine glass he'd just reached for. He raised it to his lips and took a slow, insolent sip, grateful for the alcohol. Though he normally liked the meals their cook made, tonight everything tasted like ash.

"Is that your way of wishing me happy birthday, old man?" he drawled with a half-smile.

One of the bodyguards standing around the perimeter of the dining room twitched slightly. It was an infinitesimally small move, one that most would have missed. But not Haruki. His smile widened as he clashed gazes with Renji Ogawa, the head of the Kuroda Group security team and his father's primary bodyguard.

Of all the men in the Kuroda Group, Haruki knew Ogawa loathed him the most. A traditionalist to the core, the man had always regarded Haruki's presence in the Kuroda household as an eyesore and an affront to the moral code and practices of their organization. It didn't help that his brother Riuji had perished at Yashiro's side a week ago, along with another member of the Kuroda Group security team. Ogawa was pissed as hell and looking to take his anger out on someone. Anyone.

Well, I'm not going to just stand there and take that bastard's punches if he comes at me.

Haruki's attention was distracted by his father's sigh.

Akihito Kuroda wiped his mouth with a napkin. One of the bodyguards moved his chair back as he rose to his feet.

"I had hoped that whatever respect you had for Yashiro meant that you would gracefully accept the role that is now yours."

Haruki masked a flinch at his father's dispassionate words.

"There has never been a single doubt in my mind that Yashiro was the one best suited of the two of you for the task of being my successor," his father continued in the same lifeless tone he always used when he addressed Haruki. "Today, yet again, you prove me to be correct."

Haruki clenched his teeth, his face burning with mortification and anger.

"I wish you to be my successor about as much as you wish to take on the duty," Akihito Kuroda added, his eyes cold gimlets as he stared at Haruki. "But remember this.

Neither you nor I have a choice in this matter. Our kumichō has accepted my recommendation to officially make you my heir."

Haruki startled at that. "Kanzaki-san has already agreed to my succession?"

"He has indeed." His father turned and headed for the door. "So, do me a favor. Do not dishonor our family name or the memory of your brother."

Haruki gazed blindly at his father, shock still echoing through him.

Akihito Kuroda paused in the doorway. "One more thing." He directed an arctic look at Haruki over his shoulder. "You are not to do anything so foolish and misguided as to attempt to avenge your brother's death. Dealing with the Triad is my responsibility."

Haruki stiffened.

His father narrowed his eyes. "You will do as you are told, boy. Or you will have me to answer to. Is that understood?"

Haruki bit back the sharp retort bubbling up his throat and muttered a reluctant, "Yes, sir."

He met Ogawa's chilly gaze as the latter headed after his father. He could see it in the bodyguard's eyes. The wish that almost everyone in the Kuroda Group had tonight.

That it was Haruki who had died last week instead of Yashiro.

Silence fell around him as he stared at the remains of his meal with a frown. He downed his wine, tapped the smartband on his left wrist, and brought up a number.

"Hey," he said to the guy who picked up, "I need a favor."

CHAPTER THREE

"Don't you think we should have asked him first?" Nate Conway said.

"If we play this well, he won't even realize the guy's there," Serena Blake muttered, hands resting lightly on the steering wheel of their rental car. "It's only for a week. And the mansion's basement is huge." A faint pounding sounded from the trunk. She directed a brief frown at the rearview mirror. "Besides, can you think of a safer place in the country right now?"

Nate hesitated. "I can't. Still, we *are* staying at his house."

Serena glanced at him as she took the exit onto Interstate 90. Though they were both super soldiers who had been designed in a lab with the sole purpose of becoming brutal killing machines, there was no denying that Nate possessed a kind and generous heart. It was one of the reasons Serena and Ben had always been so protective of him, even though Nate was physically bigger and stronger than either of them.

A bout of melancholy danced through her at the

thought of Ben, her and Nate's long-lost comrade in arms and the first man she had ever loved. She smiled wryly at the thought. He'd been younger than her by several years and pretty oblivious to her feelings.

Another face flashed before her eyes then. That of a man with dark hair and eyes. A man who was the complete opposite of Ben both in looks and character. Someone whose destiny was now closely linked to hers and Nate's, whether she liked it or not.

Drake Hunter. The man who had been indirectly responsible for Ben's death several years past. And the twin brother of Artemus Steele, the man whose home Serena and Nate were currently living in.

"We do have one major obstacle to overcome though, if our plan is to succeed," Serena said, trying to distract herself from the troubling feelings clouding her mind.

"The rabbit?" Nate said.

Serena nodded grimly. "The rabbit. I bet he rats on us in a heartbeat."

More pounding sounded from the trunk.

"*Will you shut the hell up back there?*" Serena shouted over her shoulder. She looked at Nate. "You sure you tied him up properly?"

"You watched me do it," Nate said, deadpan.

Serena pursed her lips. "I'm surprised that little weasel can still move. Maybe we should have used a tranquilizer."

"The last time you used a tranquilizer, the guy stopped breathing and I had to do mouth-to-mouth while you gave him the antidote," Nate mumbled.

"That wasn't my fault," Serena protested mildly. "Lou said that drug was the latest rage in mercenary world. How was I to know it was meant for hunting large mammals?"

Nate was silent for a moment. "About the rabbit."

"What about him?" Serena said.

"We could always try bribing him with his favorite food."

Serena grimaced. "Prime Kobe beef? You and I don't earn enough to buy that kind of expensive shit every day." She paused. "And I blame Callie for introducing him to Kobe beef."

"I think Artemus blames Callie too," Nate said. "At this rate, he's gonna have to raise our rent just to be able to afford to feed Smokey."

Smokey the Rex rabbit, AKA the hellhound, was another ally they had befriended three weeks ago. Serena had been surprised to discover that he and Callie Stone, the widow of one of the wealthiest men in the country and another new friend, were siblings of sorts. She sighed.

Life is just full of surprises at the moment.

Nate's smartband chimed while Serena was still pondering whether this was necessarily a bad thing or not. His face softened when he read the message that had just come through.

"Who is it?" Serena asked. She suspected she already knew the answer from Nate's expression.

"It's Callie." He smiled faintly. "She's having a meeting with her accountants. She says she's about five minutes from letting the Chimera loose and burning the place down." He chuckled. "She sent a selfie."

A reluctant grin curved Serena's lips when Nate showed her the picture. There on the screen was an impish-looking, pretty green-eyed blonde who was currently rolling her eyes and pretending to hang herself with her expensive Burberry scarf.

Just as Smokey was the Hound of Hades, so Callie had turned out to be another mythological creature, namely the fire-breathing, part-lion, part-snake, part-goat beast from ancient Lycia.

Serena passed Goose Island presently and came off the highway. She drove through several residential blocks before turning onto a private road a short distance from a public park. The lane meandered up a gentle rise to a pair of imposing, cast and wrought iron gates. A panel with a digital display slid open on the metal post on the side of the grass-lined path when Serena rolled to a stop beside it. She keyed in a code, waited for the gates to open, and pulled onto the driveway beyond.

Twilight engulfed the car as they entered a band of thick woodland. The trees soon cleared and the outlook opened up ahead.

An immense, three-story, Gothic mansion appeared on the summit of the hill, beyond the private cemetery and gardens that made up a third of the eight-acre estate. The leaded windows gracing the irregular facades of the building sparkled brightly in the light of the setting sun.

"That sight never gets old," Serena murmured as she gazed at the gable roofs with their daunting spires, the enormous stone chimneys, and the extensive decorative trimmings adorning the outlandish property.

Nate nodded in agreement.

The mansion technically belonged to the LeBlancs, one of the oldest and wealthiest families in Chicago. Charles LeBlanc, the man who would give rise to the LeBlanc dynasty, had been a close friend of Jean Baptiste Du Sable, the founding father of the 19th century settlement that would eventually become the great city of Chicago. Charles LeBlanc had also been Chicago's first blacksmith and was reputed to have been one of the best metal workers in the world at the time. It was a skill that had been passed down the generations for over two centuries until the untimely death of Karl LeBlanc, Artemus's mentor and the man he had considered his adoptive father.

Elton LeBlanc, Karl's younger brother and the last direct descendant of Charles LeBlanc, had not objected when Karl had bequeathed his antique shop and the house to Artemus in his will. Not only was Elton another mentor to Artemus and his oldest friend, he benefited immensely from Artemus's unique skills when it came to identifying the rare and unusual period pieces that came through his auction house.

They'd just pulled up next to a black SUV and a Porsche parked in front of the south-facing porch when the soft rumble of an engine rose behind them.

"Uh-oh," Nate muttered. He stared at the side mirror of their rental. "I thought they were coming back tonight."

Serena eyed the black BMW superbike racing up the driveway in the rearview mirror. "We're still good. Just act cool."

The bike slowed to a stop behind their rental car. They stepped out of the vehicle and became the focus of a pair of puzzled stares.

CHAPTER FOUR

"Hey," Artemus greeted from the back of the bike. "What's with the new wheels?"

"It's for an undercover job," Serena replied in a light tone.

Her gaze flicked to Drake as he powered down the engine and climbed off the motorcycle.

Artemus got off and studied the super soldiers' run-down, rust-covered Ford Escort with a raised eyebrow. "Well, you sure as hell chose a classic."

Hinges squeaked on the porch of the mansion. A door opened to reveal a chocolate-brown Rex rabbit. He hopped to the top of the steps and paused, nose quivering as he sniffed the air.

Artemus grinned. "What, you missed us?"

Smokey huffed and rubbed his face with his paws.

Artemus's smile faded as he listened to the words resonating inside his skull. Drake's lips twitched.

"What do you mean, did I get your Kobe beef?" Artemus asked Smokey indignantly. "No hello? No *'Hi, Art. I missed you, Art. I'm so glad to see you, Art.'* And like I already told you, only Callie can afford to buy that shit!" He narrowed his eyes. "You know, for someone who's living here without paying his dues, you sure have some nerve, buddy. Maybe we should put you to work. I hear rabbit cafes are still the rage in Japan. I reckon we should look at starting one in Chicago."

Smokey's eyes flashed red. He cocked his hind leg threateningly against one of the Victorian posts holding up the porch's roof.

"Oh God," Drake muttered. "Not this again."

Artemus straightened to his full height and levelled a menacing glare at Smokey. "Do that and you're spending the night in the mausoleum."

A metallic pounding rose in the early evening air. Serena tensed. The pounding came again, the sound gaining in urgency and volume.

Artemus, Drake, and Smokey stared at the Ford Escort.

"What's that noise?" Artemus said.

"Just something rattling under the car." Serena waved a hand vaguely in the air. "We've been hearing it on the drive all the way up here."

She shifted so she was standing in front of the Ford Escort's trunk. Nate did the same.

Lines furrowed Drake's brow. "You've got someone in there, haven't you?"

Serena bristled. "I don't know what you mean. Like I said, the car's a piece of junk and—"

A muffled shout drowned out the rest of her words.

She scowled and twisted on her heels. "Why, that little —! How the hell did he get rid of his gag?"

She glared at the trunk before glancing accusingly at Nate.

Nate sighed. "You watched me put it on him."

Artemus folded his arms across his chest and stared coldly at Serena and Nate. "Okay, what is going on here? You'd better spill before I decide to make you two spend the night in the mausoleum too."

"It's none of your business," Serena said coolly. "And may I remind you that we're paying you rent."

"You made it my damn business when you brought whomever is in there to my home," Artemus retorted.

Nate looked at Serena. "We might as well tell him. He's got that look on his face that says he's not gonna back down."

Serena hesitated. "Alright." She frowned at Artemus. "But promise me you'll let him stay the night at least."

"I'll make that decision after you explain what exactly it is you two are up to," Artemus responded mutinously.

Serena muttered something under her breath and opened the trunk.

They stared at the pale, sniveling, hog-tied man lying inside the luggage compartment of the vehicle. The duct tape over his mouth had peeled off under the sheer volume of snot and tears it had been subjected to, leaving angry, red blotches on his skin. An incoherent whimper escaped him as he gazed at them, his eyes wide with fear.

"Fuck me," Drake said dully. "Is that who I think it is?"

Artemus glanced at him. "What? You know this guy?"

Serena, Nate, and Drake turned and stared at him. The guy in the trunk looked equally shocked.

"Do you *not* watch the news?" Serena said.

"No," Artemus replied bluntly.

Drake sighed and ran a hand through his hair. "That's Kaito Sasaki. He's the sole survivor and primary witness to a violent crime that took three lives in L.A. a week ago."

Artemus blinked. "Oh." He observed the silent, petrified man watching them as if they were about to skin him and eat him alive for a moment, before directing a quizzical frown at Serena. "So, what's he doing in the trunk of your car?"

"He's currently under our protection," Serena said. "It's a favor for Lou."

Lou Flint was the super soldier who had come to their aid a few weeks back, when Callie and Nate had been taken prisoner by the secretive organization of demons they now knew as Ba'al.

Artemus arched an eyebrow. "Don't they have the FBI for stuff like that? How's Lou, by the way?"

"He's good. He's in Africa with Tom. He says hi." Serena pulled a face. "When I said it was a favor for him, I actually meant it was a job for the FBI." She cocked a thumb at Sasaki. "There have been three attempts on this guy's life in the last five days. The FBI are convinced they have a mole in their organization leaking information to the Triad, so they bundled him into a plane in the middle of the night and arranged for a pickup and private protection. He tried to make a run for it after we collected him, hence why he's in the trunk."

Artemus stiffened. "The Triad?"

"Yeah," Nate muttered. "They are the ones suspected of carrying out the murders in L.A."

"Not only that, Sasaki also has the Yakuza looking for him," Serena said.

A vein started to throb in Artemus's left temple.

"The Yakuza?" he repeated in a lifeless voice. "You mean, the Japanese mafia are also after this guy?"

"The murder victims were all Yakuza," Drake said. "Chief among them was Yashiro Kuroda, the heir to the

Kuroda Group, the biggest Yakuza organization on the West Coast."

"The Kuroda Group is itself allied to the largest Japanese crime syndicate in the world." Serena indicated the man in the trunk. "Word on the street is they're dying to question Sasaki here about the events of that night. We thought this would be the safest place to guard him until the FBI moves him to another location."

"You did, did you?" Artemus said in a low growl.

"I think he's about to blow," Nate murmured to Serena.

"He is?" she said skeptically.

"There's a vein throbbing in his temple," Drake added helpfully.

Serena stared. "That's a big vein."

Smokey took a hard look at Artemus and darted back inside the house.

CHAPTER FIVE

DANIEL DELACOURT CLIMBED OUT OF THE SWIMMING pool of his modern Bel Air mansion, headed over to a sun lounger, and poured himself a glass of champagne from the bottle sitting in an ice bucket on a sidetable.

"Report," he said coldly to the figure who stood silently watching him.

"We haven't discovered anything unusual yet, sir," the man said in a low voice. "None of the objects we've examined have demonstrated any reaction to our demonic energy."

Delacourt savored a sip of his drink and turned to gaze out over the foothills of the Santa Monica Mountains to the distant Pacific Ocean.

"Keep looking," he ordered. "I know it's there." He paused. "Any newborn fledglings?"

"No, sir."

Delacourt looked over at the demon. "Make sure to feed the ones who recently awakened well and get them strong. We're going to need more bodies on the ground with all the trouble brewing between the Triad and the Kuroda Group."

He dismissed the man and swallowed the rest of the champagne while he pondered the events of the last fortnight.

It had been ten days since Ba'al had ordered Tian Gao Lee, one of L.A.'s most notorious Triad gang leaders, to kill Yashiro Kuroda in cold blood. The execution had been as much a rite of passage for Tian Gao's admission into Ba'al as a full-fledged demon general as it had been a warning to the Kuroda Group.

Of all the criminal organizations Ba'al had subjugated and forced into working under them since they first made their presence known around the world a decade ago, the Yakuza had proven to be the toughest one yet to bring into their fold. Not only were they cunning and tenacious, their long-standing moral codes and beliefs based on centuries of tradition made them impervious to bribery and intimidation.

Yashiro Kuroda's murder was going to be a rude wakeup call for the Japanese mafia. How they chose to react in response to the violent crime would determine Ba'al's future interaction with them. That his organization could wipe out the Yakuza crime syndicates was not something Delacourt ever doubted. Ba'al was powerful and growing more so every year, especially with all the new demons awakening around the world.

But the Yakuza could prove to be very powerful allies indeed and defeating them in an all-out war would result in a blood bath that would draw far too many curious eyes toward Ba'al's activities.

Their organization had enemies and they were growing

stronger too. The recent events in New York and the death of Erik Park, one of Ba'al's most powerful demons, had proven that.

Delacourt frowned.

Killing Yashiro Kuroda had not just been about Tian Gao proving his worth to their organization or sending a clear message to the Yakuza. It had also been the quickest way for Delacourt to secure the building that had become a focus of interest for Ba'al's supreme master in the last month.

We have to find it. Before anyone else does.

HARUKI CAST A FINAL LOOK AT HIS LAPTOP, MIRRORED the screen onto his smart glasses, and got out of the car he'd parked behind a row of trees. A cold, blustery wind raced down the hillside and prickled his exposed face. He pulled his black muffler up over his mouth and nose, checked his weapons, and started up the slope.

He was at the wall of the estate in seconds.

Haruki paused in the shadows and examined the towering stone rampart before him. Up close, he could see no cameras or security sensors atop it. He narrowed his eyes.

That doesn't mean there aren't any though.

He headed west until he reached the spot he had iden-tified as the one least likely to give away his approach to the property, took a small foldable grappling hook from the pouch on his back, and was over the wall in under a minute.

Haruki landed lightly on the soft forest floor and remained rock still for a moment. Moonlight peeked through the thick band of clouds drifting overhead and washed across the woodland he stood in. He waited until gloom descended around him once more before switching his smart glasses to night mode and heading east across the grounds.

The mansion appeared between the treetops moments later, a giant, eldritch shape looming menacingly against the dark heavens. The place was pitch black but for the muted lamps on the porch and a light out back. He'd just reached the treeline and was calculating the best angle of approach across the expanse of exposed ground that separated him from the closest entry point when he sensed a presence behind him.

Haruki dropped to the ground, whipped his Beretta out, and levelled it at the head of the man who'd materialized out of the dark like a ghost.

"Shit!" He took his smart glasses off and scowled up into Renji Ogawa's cold features. "What the hell are you doing here?!"

Ogawa crouched down beside him. He glanced at the house up ahead before directing a frown at Haruki. "I could ask you the same thing, young Master."

Haruki blinked. His mouth dropped open. "What —*what did you just call me?*"

A muscle twitched in Ogawa's cheek.

"As the heir to the Kuroda Group, it is our duty to address you as such," he said in a voice that told Haruki exactly how he felt about the matter. "And I have been reassigned to your guard as of today, by order of your father. It's a good thing I had a GPS tracker installed in your smartband. So, once again, why did you slip past your escort and come here, young Master?"

Haruki glanced accusingly at the slim device on his left

wrist, swallowed the bitter words bubbling up his throat at Ogawa's patronizing tone, and looked past the bodyguard.

He swore when he saw the shadowy silhouettes around them. "Damn it! How many of you are there?"

"Six, including me," Ogawa replied icily.

Surprise darted through Haruki.

"Your father instructed me to double your guard," Ogawa said in response to his unspoken question.

Haruki clenched his jaw as understanding finally dawned.

"Really?" he said sardonically. "Was that to protect his one and only remaining heir, or his son?"

Ogawa studied him for a silent moment.

"You are more of an idiot than I thought you were," he murmured.

Haruki was about to tell the bodyguard where he could take those words and shove them when something drew his gaze. He looked toward the mansion. A light had appeared in one of the rooms facing them. A figure moved past the windows.

Haruki started to rise.

Ogawa grabbed his arm. "Where are you going?"

Haruki glared at the bodyguard. "There's someone in that house who knows what happened to Yashiro. I'm going to talk to them."

"Your method of starting a conversation seems a little extreme." Ogawa indicated the gun Haruki still gripped in his hand. "And you don't know what's waiting for you in there. This could be another trap."

Haruki slipped his smart glasses back on his face.

"There's a drone above this property right now," he said coolly. "It's armed with infrared sensors. And it's telling me there are only two people in that house. So, unless you want to explain to my father why you had to shoot me to stop me, I suggest you shut the hell up and let me get on with it."

CHAPTER SIX

SERENA LOCKED THE DOOR TO THE BEDROOM AND
dropped the key in the back pocket of her jeans. She
headed along the maze of corridors to the main staircase
landing, took the steps to the first floor, and went to
collect her bowl of warm popcorn from the kitchen. The
antique grandfather clock in the foyer chimed the hour as
she strolled through on her way to the TV room. She
dropped into a weathered Chesterfield chair, propped her
feet on a leather footstool, and grabbed the TV remote.

"Come on, guys," she muttered. "Hurry the hell up. I'm
starving here!"

She grabbed a handful of popcorn and started flicking
the TV channels absentmindedly.

Two days had passed since she and Nate had brought
Kaito Sasaki to Chicago. After he'd calmed down from his
hissy fit, Artemus had reluctantly agreed to let the man
stay for as long as was needed, a decision that had
surprised Serena and Nate as much as it had Drake.

A faint grin curved her lips.

That guy's bark is infinitely worse than his bite.

Serena's smile faded when she recalled her short conversation with Drake the day before. Artemus's visit to Kansas City had confirmed what he and Drake had suspected ever since William Boone, the father of Artemus's assistant Otis Boone, had told them of the prophecy his wife had recorded before her death. A prophecy that spoke of two brothers who would come to play a central role in some kind of future Judgement Day. Twins born of the same mother but sired by different fathers.

There was a lot Serena still found hard to believe about what she had heard in Pittsburgh a few weeks ago. But there was no denying what she had seen with her own eyes since the day her and Nate's paths had collided with Artemus and Drake's.

Evil existed in this world and it lived under the skin of ordinary men and women.

Artemus had been quieter than usual since he'd found out that the woman he'd run away from when he was sixteen wasn't his real mother. Even Smokey had given him a wide berth after he and Drake had returned from Kansas City, preferring to sleep in Callie's room instead.

Serena settled on a news channel, finished the popcorn, and got up to grab a beer from the kitchen. She'd just popped the cap and taken a swig out of the bottle when the back door opened.

"Finally," she said, closing the refrigerator. "I thought you were never going to get here."

◇

HARUKI STUDIED THE BEAUTIFUL BRUNETTE WITH PALE blue eyes staring at him from across a large kitchen with a molded ceiling, weathered wallpaper, a checkerboard-tile floor, and the biggest cast-iron range he'd ever seen. Her gaze flickered briefly to Ogawa and their men as they piled into the room behind him.

Surprise faded from the woman's gaze. She took a slow sip of her beer, her expression strangely calm.

"I gotta hand it to you," she drawled. "You guys are good. I didn't sense you at all."

Haruki looked past her to a hallway leading off the kitchen. "Where is he?"

The brunette arched an eyebrow. "Where is who?"

Haruki took a step forward, his body humming with tension. "Kaito Sasaki. I know he's here."

The brunette crossed her ankles and leaned her hip against the refrigerator. "That FBI mole must be a goddamn freakin' genius."

Haruki frowned. "What FBI mole?"

The brunette's face grew serious. "Oh. So, not the FBI mole." She narrowed her eyes slightly. "You know, you're either dumb or a reckless hothead." She paused. "Judging from the looks your men just flashed at you, I'm gonna go for the latter, Haruki Kuroda."

Haruki stiffened, conscious of Ogawa's eyes on him. "How do you know my name?"

A mocking smile curved the woman's lips. "Oh, I know a lot more than just your name, kid."

Haruki scowled at her condescending tone.

That's it!

He raised his Beretta and drew a sharp breath when it was knocked out of his grasp the next instant.

The woman was standing in front of him.

Haruki blinked. The sound of the gun clattering to the floor and skidding across the tiles echoed around the kitchen.

How?! I didn't even see her—

"Too slow, dumbass," the brunette said with a grin.

She lobbed the beer bottle at one of Haruki's men, twisted her body, and brought her left leg up in a lightning-fast hook kick. Haruki blocked her heel an inch from his right jaw, the impact sending tingles shooting down his forearm. The bottle smashed into the bodyguard on his left, hitting the hand he'd brought up protectively in front of his face. The man cursed, blood blooming on his palm where a jagged piece of glass had cut into it.

Haruki jumped back and slipped his knives out from under the cuffs of his shirt, adrenaline sending his pulse spiking. Ogawa and the others did the same, their blades glinting as they snapped them out from beneath their suit sleeves. Though they all carried guns, the Yakuza much preferred knives and hand-to-hand combat to firearms.

He could sense the same thought going through all of their minds as they stared at their adversary.

This woman is no ordinary fighter.

"Not bad," the brunette said, her pale eyes thoughtful as she brought her leg down and examined Haruki. "There aren't many people who can stop one of my kicks. Now, what say we move this somewhere more roomy?" A grimace danced across her face. "That guy will bitch like a little girl if we break anything in here."

Who is she talking—?

The brunette turned and ran out of the kitchen.

Haruki swore and went after her, Ogawa and his men on his heels. They raced down a shadowy corridor lined with dark wood paneling and moody Renaissance paint-ings, took a couple of turns, and came out into a grand foyer.

Haruki skidded to a stop a few feet inside the hallway,

saw movement out of the corner of his right eye, and dropped to the ground.

The brunette had pushed off one of the polished wood banisters of an imposing, split staircase and was already in the air.

He glimpsed her body twisting into a flawless, spinning, reverse roundhouse kick above him, rolled into a low crouch, and threw his left dagger. Ogawa inhaled sharply as the woman's foot glanced off his chest a fraction of a second after he jumped out of the way.

Haruki knew the blow would have broken the bodyguard's ribs had it made full contact.

The brunette landed lightly in the middle of the vestibule, an amused smile on her face. Her gaze dropped to where Haruki's knife had sliced through the material of her T-shirt across her midriff. A thin, red line bloomed on the shallow cut visible through the gap.

Haruki blinked.

The wound vanished just as quickly as it had appeared.

What the hell?!

The brunette looked up. Her smile faded when she saw where the dagger had ended up.

"Damn it." She stared at the oil canvas of a galleon sailing through a stormy sea sitting inside a gold, Baroque picture frame that took pride of place above a black marble mantelpiece on the opposite side of the foyer. Haruki's blade was embedded dead center in the painting. "I bet he'll raise our rent for that."

Haruki shot up and charged toward her at the same time that Ogawa and the other bodyguards moved.

The only way they were going to take her down was if they worked together.

The brunette blocked Haruki's left knee a hairbreadth

from her right loin, thrust her right elbow toward his face, and raised an eyebrow when Ogawa stopped her strike with his right hand, surprising the both of them. The bodyguard winced, the forceful contact having evidently jarred his arm.

"Very good," the woman murmured. "But still not good enough."

CHAPTER SEVEN

HARUKI GASPED AND DOUBLED OVER WHEN SOMETHING that felt like a sledgehammer slammed into his stomach. He sagged to one knee, bile rising in his throat. The brunette front kicked Ogawa in the chest. The bodyguard soared across the foyer and crashed into an old grandfather clock with a harsh grunt.

How is she moving so fast?!

The other bodyguards went flying around the vestibule as the woman danced between them, her attacks so swift her body practically blurred.

Shit! They don't stand a chance against her!

Haruki winced, clutched his midriff, and climbed to his feet. He was going to have a hell of a bruise tomorrow. That was, if he survived this fight.

The brunette paused and looked over at him from where she stood holding one of his men by the throat up against a wall to the right.

"Oh. You can still move?" She tilted her head slightly, her eyes growing pensive once more. "I could have sworn I knocked the wind out of you."

Haruki clenched his teeth and tightened his grip on his remaining dagger. He glanced at the purple-faced bodyguard thrashing feebly in her hold.

"Let him go!"

Ogawa shot him a surprised look from where he was slowly sitting up at the base of the clock.

"Alright." The brunette released the bodyguard, dusted her hands, and turned toward him.

Haruki glared at the coughing, wheezing man on his hands and knees behind her before directing a similar warning look at Ogawa and the other bodyguards.

"Stay down!" he barked. "That's a direct order!"

A scowl darkened Ogawa's face.

The brunette slipped a dagger out from her back and headed toward Haruki. "You really think you can beat me on your own?" Her eyes glittered coldly. "Well, I'm gonna come at you with everything I've got, so don't hold back, kid."

Haruki moved his right foot behind him, widened his stance, and braced himself, the flat part of his blade flush against his left forearm.

The brunette slowed and assessed him with something that looked like admiration on her face. "You're one stubborn sonofabitch, you know that?"

The front door opened on a blast of cold air. An attractive blonde in a camel cashmere coat walked in. She released the handle of the case she was dragging behind her, pushed the door shut, and brushed her windswept hair out of her face.

"Christ, it's cold enough to freeze the balls off a brass monkey out there." She turned and grew still as she took in the scene before her. Her green eyes rounded. "Hmm."

Haruki's gaze clashed with hers. His heart thumped

hard as an uncanny sense of awareness washed over him. He blinked, unsure if he'd just glimpsed the same reaction in the blonde's expression.

An appreciative smile curved the woman's lips as she studied him. "Hello. You're hot."

The brunette rolled her eyes hard at the blonde. "Jesus, can you stop flirting for one goddamn minute? I'm in the middle of a situation here."

Voices rose from the back of the mansion.

"Hey, Serena?" a male voice called out. "Did Callie just get back? We passed a limo on the way home."

Three men carrying pizza boxes and Chinese takeout containers appeared in the corridor leading to the kitchen, a chocolate-colored rabbit hopping between their feet. They came to an abrupt halt.

The blond man in the lead stared. "What the—?"

Haruki's heart throbbed violently once more. Before he could analyze the unsettling feeling blasting through his consciousness, he glimpsed motion out the corner of his eye. Ogawa was moving toward the blonde by the door. Haruki's eyes widened when he grasped the man's intent.

"*Don't!*" he shouted at the bodyguard.

The brunette took a step forward. "Nate, stop! He can't hurt—"

Haruki started running at the same time that the giant man with the flinty eyes standing behind the rabbit raised a gun at Ogawa. The muzzle flashed, the blast of the bullet bursting forth from the barrel booming like thunder around the vestibule.

Something shifted deep inside Haruki as he dashed past the brunette with the dagger and jumped in front of the bodyguard. His stomach lurched.

Am I going to die?

Time slowed. Sound faded. The hallway blurred into a grotesque caricature of frozen, faceless figures.

In that moment, Haruki saw two things. The rabbit's eyes glowed red. And, by the door, the blonde's glittered with an emerald light.

Heat erupted inside Haruki. It rushed down his right arm to his hand. The ruby eyes of the metal dragon on the bracelet flashed crimson.

Someone gasped.

Haruki startled, sound and sight returning with the thunderous crash of blood pounding inside his skull. He was standing in front of Ogawa with his right arm stretched out before him. And, by some sort of miracle, neither of them appeared to be dead.

It took another second for him to realize everyone was staring at his right hand. He followed their stunned gazes to the bracelet on his wrist and felt his entire world tilt sideways.

There, gripped in the jaws of the dragon head that had trebled in size, was the bullet.

The slug clattered to the marble floor as the dragon spat it out, smoke curling faintly from around its nostrils and jaws. It shrank back down to its original size in the next instant, its ruby eyes glinting faintly for a second.

Haruki's knees nearly gave out beneath him.

"Did that just happen?" the blond man on the other side of the vestibule said suspiciously in the shocked silence. He waved a takeout container at the dark-haired guy beside him. "Hey, Drake. You saw that, right?"

The man called Drake nodded, his hooded gaze focused unblinkingly on Haruki.

"Young Master Haruki." Ogawa came around Haruki and hesitated before laying a hand on his shoulder. "Are you—" he swallowed convulsively, his face pale, "are you okay?"

Haruki felt the blood suddenly drain from his head. Sweat broke out across his brow. He raised his left hand to his mouth, a wave of nausea flooding him.

"Uh-oh," the blonde in the cashmere coat said. "I know that look."

"I'm gonna hurl," Haruki mumbled.

He turned, spotted something that would do, and rushed toward it.

"Hey! Hey, stop right there!" the blond man across the way said threateningly as he started to cross the vestibule. "Don't you dare—"

The sound of violent heaving and retching filled the hallway.

"—throw up in my Qing Dynasty vase," the blond man finished in a leaden voice while Haruki emptied the contents of his stomach inside the porcelain vessel sitting on a console table. There was a pause. "Is that a *knife* in the middle of my goddamn painting?!"

The brunette sighed. "I can explain."

CHAPTER EIGHT

"What the hell was that?" Haruki Kuroda said, staring at the bracelet lying on the kitchen table.

Artemus swallowed down a bite of egg-fried rice with sweet-and-sour chicken before pointing his chopsticks at the item in question. "*That*, my friend, was the manifestation of an object of power."

He leaned against the kitchen counter and studied the frowning young man sitting at the head of the table.

The Kuroda heir's bodyguards stood close to their master. They'd refused Callie's offer of pizza and drinks and were observing the other occupants of the room with suspicious eyes. Artemus hid a grimace.

Considering they're the ones who broke into this place, that's kinda insulting.

Haruki dragged his gaze from the bracelet and looked at Artemus.

"What do you mean, an object of power?" he said, clearly puzzled.

Artemus sighed, put his takeout container down, and pulled his switchblade from the back of his boot. A wave of warmth flowed down his arm from the wing marks on his back.

It had been a couple of weeks since he'd become conscious that he could draw on his power much faster and much easier than he had ever been able to do before. He suspected it was the same for Drake, Callie, and even Smokey.

Is it because of what happened to us in New York?

The knife shapeshifted smoothly into a double-edged sword. It wasn't the weapon's ultimate form. Not by any means.

Haruki shot to his feet, the chair falling behind him with a loud clatter.

"*Kokumajutsu!*" Renji Ogawa spat out, his hand rising to the butt of his gun in the holster inside his suit jacket.

The other bodyguards similarly reached for their weapons, their faces pale.

"Hey now, calm down," Drake told the nervous men in a soothing voice. He lowered his slice of pizza to his plate and narrowed his eyes at Artemus. "And you. Could you be more, I don't know, *subtle?*"

Artemus shrugged. "This was the fastest way to make my point."

The sword shrank back down to a switchblade. He tucked it inside his boot.

"What does *koku—kokuma—*that word he just said mean?" Callie asked Haruki curiously while the latter pulled his chair up and slowly took his seat again.

"Black magic," Serena murmured.

Nate frowned where he stood beside her at the range. He hadn't touched his food and was watching Haruki and the bodyguards with open distrust.

Callie's face cleared. "Oh! Don't worry," she told Ogawa. "We're not into that. We're the good guys."

"The good guys?" Haruki repeated, his expression still stunned from what he'd just witnessed.

Callie smiled and nodded. "Uh-huh. You know, like the opposite of evil."

Haruki looked unconvinced by her statement.

"MAY I?" ARTEMUS SAID.

He strolled to the table and indicated the bracelet.

Haruki hesitated before dipping his chin, his pulse hammering in his veins.

It was nearly midnight. Much to his surprise, Artemus Steele, the owner of the mansion he'd broken into and the man who'd just made a knife transform into a sword as if it were a common daily occurrence, had invited him and his escort to stay for a chat.

Haruki wasn't sure what shocked him the most. The fact that Artemus hadn't called the cops on them. What had happened in the foyer a short while back, when his bracelet had morphed into something that defied belief. Or the feeling currently coursing through him.

The same feeling that had shaken him to the core when he'd first seen Callie Stone, the blonde who'd walked through the front door moments into his fight with Serena Blake, the brunette who'd beaten the shit out of him and his men. The same feeling that had made his soul tremble when he'd laid eyes on Artemus Steele, Drake Hunter, and the rabbit called Smokey.

Affinity. Familiarity. Kinship.

Whatever it was, it was telling Haruki that he knew

these people, somehow. That he had known them for a long, long time. That there was some kind of bond between them. Which was, of course, crazy.

He'd never laid eyes on them before in his life.

Artemus lifted the bracelet and examined it carefully. He ran his fingers over the beads and paused when he touched the dragon head.

"What is it?" Callie said.

Artemus raised his head and stared at Haruki, his expression inscrutable. "Nothing." He handed the bracelet back to Haruki. "Where did you get this?"

Haruki startled when the beads touched his palm. For a second, they felt hot against his skin.

It's probably because he was holding it.

A faint crunch of bones came from his right, distracting him for an instant. He looked over to where Smokey was sitting on the counter and munching his way through an entire rotisserie chicken, his chocolate eyes radiating an intelligence and awareness that was other-worldly.

Haruki couldn't help but feel that the creature, whatever the hell he was, could read his mind.

"My brother bought it for me for my twenty-fifth birthday." He hesitated before slipping the bracelet back onto his wrist. "He got it in Hong Kong, about a month ago."

"Yashiro Kuroda?" Serena said.

Haruki's heart twisted with a now familiar pain at his brother's name. "Yes."

"Do you know where he purchased it from?" Artemus said insistently.

Haruki shook his head. "No. But I'm sure I can find out."

He glanced at Ogawa. The bodyguard nodded, his expression troubled.

"I would be grateful if you could," Artemus murmured.

Haruki studied the blond man for a moment before sighing and running a hand through his hair, his mind a maelstrom of thoughts. Yashiro's face swam before his eyes and reminded him once more why he was in Chicago in the first place.

"I don't get any of this. Any of what just happened here tonight. And I don't think I want to, quite frankly." Haruki's gaze shifted to Serena and Nate Conway, the giant man who'd shot at Ogawa. "I can tell you two are mercs," he said, his voice hardening. "Which can only mean the FBI charged you to take care of Sasaki. I need to talk to him."

"No can do," Serena said in a steely voice.

Haruki scowled. "If I discovered his location this easily, then you can bet your ass the Triad won't be far behind. I want to know what happened to my brother before somebody puts a bullet through our lawyer's head."

"What lawyer?" Callie said, puzzled. She glanced from Serena to Nate. "What's he talking about?"

Serena sighed. "It's a long story." She frowned at Haruki. "By the way, how did you know he was here? You said it wasn't the FBI mole who's been leaking information to the Triad who told you his whereabouts."

"I have my sources," Haruki said evasively.

His years at Stanford hadn't just equipped him with one of the best business degrees in the world and the network of contacts he needed to break away from the Kuroda Group. It had also introduced him to the dark web, a place where anything had a price.

"Let him talk to the guy," Artemus said.

Everyone stared at him.

"What?" Serena said.

"Let him talk to Sasaki," Artemus repeated.

"That would be a direct violation of our contract with the FBI," Nate protested.

Artemus shrugged. "What the FBI doesn't know won't hurt them."

"You're being remarkably nonchalant considering this case is going to federal court," Drake said sternly.

"Something tells me we're all going to want to hear what the lawyer has to say," Artemus murmured, his thoughtful gaze on Haruki.

CHAPTER NINE

KAITO SASAKI LOOKED LIKE HE WAS GOING TO BE SICK.

Drake felt a wave of pity for the man as he watched him face Haruki at the kitchen table.

The lawyer had barely eaten or slept since Serena and Nate had picked him up from a private airstrip outside Springfield two days ago and brought him to Artemus's mansion. Considering what the guy had witnessed and who he had looking for him, Drake wasn't surprised.

Yet, it wasn't fear he saw in the haggard man's eyes. It was shame and what looked a lot like remorse.

A muscle jumped in Haruki's cheek as he observed the last person to have seen his brother alive.

"It's okay," Serena told Sasaki where she stood beside him. "You don't have to talk if you don't want to."

Sasaki hesitated before shaking his head. "I—No. I need to do this."

Drake's eyes widened when Sasaki suddenly jumped out of his chair and prostrated himself on his knees in front of Haruki.

"I am sorry I failed to report to the Kuroda Group,

Master Haruki!" Sasaki said, his voice trembling. "And I am so, so terribly sorry about the death of Master Yashiro and our men!"

Haruki blinked, the same astonishment reverberating around the room displayed clearly on his face. He hesitated before climbing slowly to his feet.

"You don't have to do that," he told the lawyer gruffly, helping the man off the floor and back into his chair. "All I want to know is what happened the night my brother and his bodyguards were killed."

Sasaki sniffed and swallowed, close to tears. Artemus grabbed a bottle of bourbon from a cabinet and poured the man a generous shot.

"Thank you," the lawyer murmured.

They waited while he took a sip of his drink and wiped his sweat-covered brow with a handkerchief.

"I—I was on my way out of the office when Master Yashiro came to collect me that day," Sasaki started in a shaky voice. "He said he had someone interested in buying a piece of prime real estate he had purchased the month before in Downtown L.A. Someone who was willing to pay more than double the price it had originally been valued at. I was familiar with the details of the deal, so he requested I come along and bring the deeds. We—we drove to a warehouse at the end of an abandoned pier, in the port."

Haruki leaned forward, his forearms on the table. "What happened when you got there?"

"The place was deserted," Sasaki said. "Or so we thought at first. We couldn't see any vehicles out front. Judging from Master Yashiro's demeanor and the exchange he had with Mr. Ogawa, his bodyguard, they were wary of the choice of location."

"That stupid brother of mine," Ogawa muttered stiffly, his eyes dark with pain. "I told him to always trust his instincts."

Serena raised an eyebrow. "Riuji Ogawa was your brother?"

"Yes," Haruki replied quietly in Ogawa's stead. "Riuji used to take care of Yashiro and I, way back when we still lived in Kyushu. He was...family."

"So, you went inside the warehouse?" Drake asked the lawyer.

Sasaki nodded, color slowly draining from his glistening face as he gazed blindly into his glass of bourbon. "I was the last one in. I stayed back a bit, which is why I think I went unnoticed for as long as I did."

The glass rattled on the table as his hands started to shake.

"What did you see?" Artemus said.

"There were men waiting for us inside the building," Sasaki mumbled. He raised a hand to his eyes, as if to block out what he had witnessed that day. "It was dark at first. Then, they turned a light on. Master Yashiro seemed relaxed as he approached them, but I could tell Mr. Ogawa and the other bodyguard were nervous. Master Yashiro greeted the leader of the group as if he knew the man well. They exchanged a couple of pleasantries. And then Master Yashiro said they should talk about the reason for their meeting."

Sasaki lowered his hand.

A sudden foreboding danced through Drake as he studied Sasaki's terrified gaze. He glanced at Artemus and saw the blond watching the lawyer unblinkingly. So were Smokey and Callie.

"That was when everything changed." A low sob rose

in Sasaki's throat. "That was when those men turned into
—into *monsters!*"

SERENA EXCHANGED A STARTLED GLANCE WITH NATE AS
a stunned silence fell across the kitchen.

Wait. Does he—?

"What do you mean, monsters?" Haruki said in a low
voice, his knuckles white where he'd clasped his hands
together.

"They—they transformed!" Sasaki stammered. "That's
the only way I can describe what I saw. The air became
heavy, as if all the oxygen was being sucked out of the
room. Then, those men—those men's bodies changed! The
whites of their eyes turned black and their pupils became
circles of yellow light. Then, their—" the lawyer shuddered, "their fingers and toes grew into claws! And their
faces!" Sasaki closed his eyes tightly. "Oh God, their faces!"

Shit.

Serena looked over at Drake, her body stiff with
sudden tension. A muscle was dancing in the man's jawline.
Her gaze switched to Artemus.

To her surprise, the blond did not look in the least bit
shocked by what he was hearing.

Did he know?

"What did they do to Yashiro and our men?" Haruki
asked in a deathly still tone.

Sasaki faltered, a pleading look dawning on his face.

"Tell them," Artemus said to the lawyer. He glanced at
Haruki and his escort. "They deserve to hear the truth."

As Sasaki finally described the grim details of what
Yashiro Kuroda and his two bodyguards had endured that

day, Serena knew for certain that whatever had happened in L.A. had something to do with Ba'al. She could tell from the others' expressions that they thought the same.

This was too big to be a random demonic attack. The fact that the target had been a prominent member of the Yakuza meant that it had likely been a deliberate ambush.

Elton LeBlanc and his team of Vatican agents had unearthed some of the activities of the New York branch of Ba'al after they had defeated them in an epic battle in Manhattan just over two weeks ago. Chief among those had been Ba'al's modus operandi when it came to subjugating the criminal groups whose territories they wanted to take over.

"I ran away from the building and hid in a nearby storage container," Sasaki mumbled. "I could hear them looking for me, but they didn't find me. I was picked up by a police officer who was driving past the docks an hour later. I—I am ashamed to say that I was so terrified by what I had witnessed that I told him who I was working for and what had just transpired. It was only afterward that I was told the bodies were no longer in the warehouse."

Serena frowned. Yashiro Kuroda's mutilated remains and those of his men had been discovered floating in the sea by a patrol boat, some half a mile from the coastline.

A strained hush descended around them after the lawyer stopped talking. Judging from the looks on the faces of Haruki's men, several of them wanted to throw up.

"Name," Haruki said in a lifeless voice. "What is the name of the man Yashiro went to meet?"

Sasaki hesitated. "Tian—Tian Gao Lee."

Haruki took a shuddering breath, rage darkening his

eyes and his fingers curling into fists. Low mumbles broke out among his pale-faced bodyguards. They obviously knew who Lee was.

"Those things you saw were demons," Artemus told Sasaki quietly. "We fought against them here, in Chicago, and in New York a few weeks ago."

HARUKI UNFROZE WHERE HE'D BEEN SITTING AS STILL AS stone while he listened to Kaito Sasaki's gruesome account of the violent murder of his brother and their men. He turned his head stiffly and stared at Artemus, his blood thundering in his veins. Ogawa similarly moved where he stood gripping the back of Haruki's chair, the fury emanating off him resonating with Haruki's own rage.

Drake narrowed his eyes at Artemus. "Should we really be talking about this with them?"

"Yes," Artemus replied. He looked from Drake to Serena and Nate. "I thought I sensed something when you brought Sasaki here. A faint trace of demonic energy. I suspected he'd had some kind of contact with them."

Understanding dawned on Serena's face. "Is that why you let him stay?"

Artemus dipped his chin. He turned to Sasaki. "I think the real reason they couldn't find you that night is the charm you carry with you."

The lawyer startled. "My omamori?"

He hesitated before reaching inside his shirt and removing a small, colorful, rectangular silk bag at the end of a rope necklace.

"It's a powerful protective amulet," Artemus said. "I can tell without touching it."

"It was given to me by my grandmother before I left Tokyo," Sasaki said, his expression shocked. "She had it made for me at our family's Shinto shrine."

"Well, thank your grandmother the next time you see her," Artemus said drily. "Your ancestors were most definitely with you that night. You'd be a dead man if it wasn't for that charm."

Haruki slowly rose to his feet, his pulse racing and a thousand questions storming his mind.

"How do you know?" he said in a low voice. "How do you know these things? How did you know about Sasaki's *omamori?!* And those men you call—*demons!* What do you know about them?!"

Artemus glanced at his comrades. "Like I said, we've gone up against them before."

His next words caused Haruki's eyes to widen in surprise.

"They were the ones who killed the man I considered my father."

CHAPTER TEN

CALLIE MUFFLED A YAWN BEHIND HER HAND AND descended the mansion's main staircase with Smokey. She was about to follow the smell of freshly brewed coffee to the kitchen when she stopped and gazed in the direction of the TV room. She hesitated before crossing the foyer on tip-toes and peering inside.

What are we doing?

Callie looked down into Smokey's curious eyes and placed a finger against her lips. She padded barefoot across the room, glided soundlessly past the bodyguard sleeping in an armchair next to the fireplace, and stopped in front of the leather couch beneath the bay windows.

Haruki lay on his side with his arms folded across his chest, his ribcage moving gently under a light fleece blanket with his slow, steady breathing. A faint frown furrowed his brow even in sleep.

Although Artemus had offered the young Yakuza heir and his bodyguards rooms for the night, the mansion being more than big enough to accommodate all of them, Haruki had insisted on taking the couch in the TV room.

Ogawa had stayed by his master's side while the rest of their men took turns guarding the mansion. Callie smiled faintly.

Not that this place needs guarding.

Her smile faded as she studied Haruki. She knelt by the couch and carefully placed her hand just above the sleeping man's heart. She closed her eyes and concentrated.

The Chimera inside her stirred languidly once more, just as it had done yesterday when she had first seen Haruki. She opened her eyes and glanced at Smokey.

"You can feel something too, can't you?" she said softly.

Smokey's nose twitched. *Yes.*

Callie studied Haruki's handsome features pensively. Her gaze shifted to the blanket. She pursed her lips, carefully lifted the top edge, and peeked beneath it.

I do not think that is a good idea, sister.

Callie ignored Smokey.

"What are you doing?" someone said behind them.

Ogawa awoke with a start.

Haruki's eyes snapped open. His hand rose instinctively to grab Callie's wrist. He released it when he saw her and sat up, a confused expression washing across his face as he glanced from her to Smokey. His gaze moved past them to the doorway.

Callie rose to her feet and looked innocently at Serena where the latter stood leaning against the doorjamb, a suspicious expression on her face and a cup of coffee in hand.

"Nothing," Callie said brightly. "Just making sure our guest was comfortable."

Smokey rolled his eyes and hopped toward the doorway.

"What's going on?" someone mumbled drowsily.

Artemus appeared behind the super soldier, his mouth open on a yawn that he barely masked with his hand, his tousled hair sticking out at crazy angles. He scratched his midriff sleepily under his T-shirt and sweatpants.

"Callie was checking Haruki out," Serena said wryly.

Ogawa froze in the act of rising from the armchair. Haruki's eyes widened. Callie grinned.

Artemus frowned at her. "You hussy." He looked down at Smokey, now sat by his feet. "And you, why don't you do something about your sister?"

Smokey let out an irritated huff.

Footsteps rose in the foyer behind them. Drake came into view. Like Serena, he was already dressed for the day.

"Nate wants to know how many pancakes he should make." He paused. "What's up?"

Serena turned and headed for the kitchen. "Kuroda's virtue was under threat. It's a good thing I turned up, otherwise the poor kid would have gotten molested in his sleep."

"You know, I don't think I'm that much younger than you," Haruki called out coldly after the super soldier.

Drake studied Callie with a look akin to pity. "You seriously need to get some, lady."

Callie's grin faded. She swallowed nervously.

"Hmm, look," she mumbled, "no offense. I mean, you're pretty good looking and you have that tall, dark, brooding thing down to a T, but you're seriously not my—"

"I didn't mean me!" Drake snapped. "And you," he glared at Artemus, "wipe that stupid smile off your face!"

He twisted on his heels and stormed after Serena.

Callie studied Artemus pensively. "'Morning, handsome." She raked his figure with her gaze. "You're looking mighty fine today."

Artemus's grin faded. "I've said it before and I'll say it again. My body is off limits."

"Aww, don't be shy," Callie cajoled.

"What is wrong with you people?" Haruki said dully.

Ogawa's stiff expression suggested he was thinking the same thing.

"You'll get used to it," Artemus said. "Want some coffee?"

ELTON LEBLANC STARED AT THE MAN ON THE VIDEOLINK on his computer screen. "Are you sure?"

"Yes," Archbishop Holmes said quietly. "It appears Ba'al was trying to hide what was happening, but some of their newborns caused quite the mess when they awoke. Our agents picked up on a sudden spike in unusual incidents from local news." Lines furrowed the older man's brow. He leaned forward, elbows on his desk and hands clasped thoughtfully under his chin. "There's one more thing, Elton. We believe the pattern we're seeing resembles what we think took place in Jerusalem, before they found it."

Isabelle Mueller shifted next to him and exchanged a tense look with Mark Daniels and Shamus Carmichael.

Elton drummed his fingers distractedly on the armrest of his chair. "Have you made any progress with Catherine Boone's journals?"

Archbishop Holmes shook his head, his expression regretful. "Unfortunately, no. William Boone did an excellent job of translating what he did. We have deciphered a few pages here and there, but they contain random information that does not seem to make much sense as of yet." He paused. "Miss Mueller and Mr. Daniels already know this, but we have asked the Immortal Societies' top experts on theology and linguistics for their assistance in this matter."

Unease rose inside Elton.

Over two weeks had passed since the battle with Erik Park and the New York branch of the sinister organization they now knew as Ba'al. It was during that fight that Mark Daniels, a long-standing Vatican agent and member of Elton's team, had died in front of their eyes, only to come back to life like the proverbial daisy a few minutes later.

Serena, Nate, and the other super soldiers who had come to their aid that day already seemed to know about the existence of these so-called Immortals. From what Elton had been able to deduce, the Immortals had been directly involved in the creation of the super soldier race Serena and Nate belonged to. And it seemed the Vatican had been aware of the existence of both the Immortals and the super soldiers for some time too.

Despite the Vatican's reassurances on the subject, Elton remained troubled. From his point of view, both the Immortals and the super soldiers were still unknown entities. He swallowed a sigh.

As if the world wasn't strange enough as it is.

CHAPTER ELEVEN

HARUKI PUT HIS KNIFE AND FORK DOWN.

"That was good," he said grudgingly, looking at the man who'd made the breakfast spread laid out across the kitchen table.

"Best pancakes ever, dude," one of his bodyguards mumbled, giving Nate a thumbs-up while he swallowed his last bite of the fluffy, grilled batter.

"Thank you," Nate murmured.

The giant man seemed to have loosened up slightly in the presence of Haruki and his men this morning, although Haruki could still see a hint of distrust in his eyes.

Probably because Ogawa went for the blonde. He glanced at the brunette seated at the table. *And I still don't know what he and Serena are.*

He was convinced the two mercenaries were more than they seemed. For one thing, Serena had brought him and his men to their knees without so much as breaking a sweat yesterday. For another, there was the fact that the wound he'd inflicted on her with his knife had healed as swiftly as it had appeared. He hadn't asked the brunette about that startling observation yet. That her explanation might end up being as fantastical as all the other things he'd heard last night was what had stopped him from voicing the question. He'd had enough crazy in the last twelve hours to last him a lifetime.

A chewing noise drew his gaze to the window seat, where Smokey was perched. The creature was busy devouring a plate stacked with sausage and bacon with great contentment.

"I thought rabbits were herbivores," Haruki muttered.

"He's special," Callie said with a smile.

Drake sighed. Artemus took a sip of his coffee and maintained a diplomatic silence.

Haruki narrowed his eyes slightly at Callie. "Artemus said you and the rabbit are related. What did he mean by that? How can he—" he glanced at Smokey, "be your sibling?"

"Life is full of weird and wonderful mysteries," Callie said wisely.

Haruki frowned. "Are you mocking me?"

Callie wrinkled her nose at him. "You're way too cute for that."

Haruki felt his ears grow warm. Cute was not a term he had ever associated with himself. A muffled snort sounded behind him. He looked over his shoulder and glared at one of his bodyguards.

"Callie's right," Artemus said. "Smokey is...special. Besides, I would have thought you'd seen enough last night to convince you that the world is not as straightforward as you think it is."

Haruki sat back and studied the blond man and his friends with a carefully neutral expression. He still hadn't fully digested all the far-fetched things he'd heard and seen yesterday. And there was a lot he remained skeptical about. One thing he was certain of though.

These people were not your average, run-of-the-mill folks.

I can't think about that right now. I have to get back to L.A. and find Tian Gao Lee.

Haruki rose to his feet, his resolve unshaken. After all, the only reason he'd come to Chicago was to find a lead to his brother's murderer.

"Thank you for your hospitality and for not calling the cops on us," he told Artemus. "We'll be on our way." He looked over at Serena and Nate. "Say goodbye to Sasaki for me." Haruki hesitated. "And thank him. For everything."

THEY WATCHED THE SUVS DISAPPEAR DOWN THE driveway.

Callie glanced at Artemus. "You're just going to let him leave?"

Serena frowned faintly, puzzled by the undercurrent of tension in her voice.

Artemus shrugged. "I don't exactly have a choice in the matter, do I? He's a grown man. And, right now, he only has one thing on his mind."

"He'll die if he goes up against the Triad on his own," Drake said, his tone equally troubled. "Especially if they have demons on their side."

"Like I said, the guy's a grown man," Artemus murmured, the thoughtful lines wrinkling his brow belying his casual tone.

"Why are you so interested in Kuroda?" Serena asked

curiously. "The demon stuff I get. And that bracelet thing was just weird." She glanced between Callie and Drake. "It seems to me there's more to it than that."

Callie hesitated and looked at Smokey. "We felt something yesterday. When we met Haruki. Or at least the Chimera did." Her gaze shifted to Artemus and Drake. "You felt it too, didn't you?"

The two men remained silent.

"Felt what?" Serena asked with narrowed eyes.

The sound of an engine rose in the distance, distracting them. They looked across the yard to the drive. A black town car came into view. It pulled up smoothly in front of the mansion.

"Now what?" Artemus muttered.

A tall, burly man with gray-flecked hair and a beard got out of the vehicle.

"Who was that we just passed?" Elton LeBlanc called out.

"No one you know," Artemus said grouchily.

"Jeez, someone's a grump this morning," Isabelle said, stepping out of the vehicle with Shamus and Mark.

"Yeah, well, that's because someone's getting instant bad vibes about whatever it is you're here for," Artemus grumbled.

Smokey's nose twitched in agreement.

Elton climbed the porch steps, an affable smile on his face. "Come now, can't a man visit his friends?"

"Oh." Serena raised an eyebrow. "Are we friends now?"

"You stole the words right out of my mouth," Drake murmured.

Elton's smile faded. "You know this place is partly mine, right?"

Nate sighed. "I'll go make some coffee."

Artemus stared. "What?"

"I want you to come to L.A. with us," Elton repeated. He looked around the kitchen. "I would like all of you to accompany us, actually."

"What for?" Serena asked.

Elton's expression grew somber. "Rome got in touch this morning. They want us to investigate a recent rise in demonic manifestation in L.A. Several Vatican agents have gone missing after they went to check out possible demonic sightings."

Artemus exchanged a surprised look with Drake. He could tell his brother was thinking the same thing.

"L.A., huh?" he murmured. "Man, that city is demon central right now."

Elton looked puzzled. "What do you mean?"

"Just something we heard on the grapevine," Artemus said dismissively. "Anyway, why do you want *us* to come with you? The Vatican has more than enough people to deal with whatever is going on in L.A."

"You said it yourself a few weeks ago. You, Drake, Callie, and Smokey can sense demons. No one in our organization can do that." Elton studied Artemus with a calculating expression. "Besides, I thought you wanted to find out about Ba'al and your own origins. This is the perfect opportunity for you to do just that."

Artemus frowned at the blatant bait.

He's right. The only reason Drake and Callie are living here is to figure out why we possess the powers that we do and what our weapons were intended for. His gaze shifted briefly to Serena and Nate. *And their Fate is linked to ours too, whether they like it or not.*

Artemus hesitated for a moment longer before blowing out a sigh. "Alright. We'll come to L.A."

Elton blinked. "What, just like that? No arguments? No demands? No *'Hell no, Elton!'*?" He narrowed his eyes. "Are you feeling okay?"

Artemus scowled. "I changed my mind."

"No backsies," Elton countered smugly.

Drake crossed his arms and directed a grim stare at Artemus. "I hope you weren't speaking for all of us there, Goldilocks. I haven't agreed to this."

"Neither have we," Serena said, her expression similarly aloof.

"The Vatican will pay you generously for your services," Elton told the two mercenaries and the thief.

"When do we leave?" Drake said smoothly.

A sardonic smile curved Serena's lips. "Wow. Money really *can* buy you anything." She ignored Drake's glare and turned to Elton. "However attractive that offer sounds, I'm afraid Nate and I will have to bow out for now. We're in the middle of a job."

Artemus looked questioningly at Callie.

The blonde grinned. "Of course I'll come! Besides, this is L.A. we're talking about. The city of sun, sea, and bronzed hotties!"

"We're going there on a mission, not for a vacation," Artemus said with a sigh. "And may I remind you that your dearly beloved husband only died, like, four weeks ago?"

Callie ignored him and looked brightly at Smokey. "So, how many bikinis do you think I should bring?"

CHAPTER TWELVE

Haruki swallowed a bite of his burger with his beer and kept his eyes on the strip club one hundred and twenty feet across the junction from where he sat at a window seat inside a diner.

Door chimes jingled on his left. Someone entered the restaurant. A man sat down next to him a moment later, a glass of water in hand.

Haruki sighed, put his burger down, and wiped his hands with a napkin.

"How the hell did you find me?" he muttered, his gaze still on the building with flashing neon lights on the other side of the intersection.

"You should know our group has eyes everywhere," Ogawa murmured.

Haruki glanced at him, unconvinced by his words.

"Let me guess," he said, his tone scathing. "There's a GPS tracker in my shoe."

Ogawa hesitated. "Belt buckle."

Haruki looked at the offending item with a disgusted

expression. "Shit. You guys really need to learn to respect people's privacy."

"Heirs to large Yakuza organizations don't have that luxury," Ogawa retorted.

Haruki stiffened.

Damn it. I keep forgetting about that.

He popped some chips into his mouth and took another sip of his beer. "Did you guys use to track my brother's every move too?"

Ogawa sniffed. "Fortunately, young Master Yashiro had a strong sense of duty and responsibility. There was no need to spy on him."

Haruki scowled. "Hey, you saying I don't have a strong sense of duty and responsibility?"

Ogawa arched an eyebrow and looked pointedly around the diner.

"Okay, present situation notwithstanding," Haruki snapped.

Ogawa wavered. "You are more...unpredictable than your brother," he said finally. "Master Yashiro was level-headed and calm."

Haruki stared at him for a moment. "You know, both you and dad make Yashiro out to be some kind of saint. That guy made me watch my first AV when I was twelve."

Ogawa choked on his water.

"So, what are you doing here?" the bodyguard said once he got his breath back.

Haruki sobered. "Waiting for someone to come out of that place."

He indicated the strip club with a jerk of his chin.

"Who, exactly?" Ogawa said.

"One of Tian Gao's men."

Ogawa frowned. "You're not really thinking of going

after him, are you? I gave the information Sasaki conveyed to us to your father when we got home this afternoon. It's up to him as the head of the Kuroda Group to decide what to do with it."

"Yeah, well, this is where my father and I differ, you see. I don't believe in pussyfooting around the subject." Haruki narrowed his eyes at Ogawa. "Tian Gao killed my brother in cold blood. I'm not waiting around to see what diplomatic solution my dad reaches with the head of the L.A. Triad. I will take him down myself, even if it costs me my life."

Ogawa's eyes darkened with frustration. "You're such a pain in the—"

Haruki straightened in his seat, his gaze locked on the building across the intersection. "There he is."

Ogawa turned and stared at the man who'd just walked out of the strip club.

JIANG FEI HONG STUMBLED SLIGHTLY WHILE HE PATTED his pockets in search of his car keys.

He was dimly aware that he was way over the drink driving limit and should call one of his subordinates to come pick him up, but the buzz of alcohol had dampened his ability to think logically three beers ago.

Metal jingled under his fingers as he tottered between rows of cars in the parking lot where he'd left his ride. He pulled his keys out and cursed when they slipped from his fingers and dropped to the ground.

He squatted down with some difficulty and was patting the blacktop under the vehicle next to him when a shadow blocked out what little light illuminated the darkened lot.

Jiang Fei squinted at the two figures looming over him. He scowled. "What the hell do you fuckers want?"

The last thing he saw was a fist heading toward his face.

TIAN GAO REACHED FOR THE CIGARETTES ON THE nightstand and lit one up.

The woman next to him panted and trembled, her naked body shiny with sweat and covered with marks and bruises that would fade by the day's end. She opened her obsidian eyes and studied him with a languid expression filled with lust.

Tian Gao leaned down and took her mouth in a brutal kiss hard enough to break the soft skin of her lips. She shuddered and let out a low guttural sound as he tasted her acrid black blood with his tongue.

Tian Gao smiled savagely. His sex drive had always been high, even when he'd been a human. Now that he was a demon, it was insatiable.

This was seemingly a characteristic of higher level demons, something he'd learned only recently. Just as he'd discovered that human females could not withstand the act of intercourse with a man possessed by a demon.

Unfortunately, it had cost several prostitutes their lives before the man who'd initiated him into Ba'al told him this.

Tian Gao now had a choice of demonic escorts at his disposal to use as he wished. Women who bore lower level demons inside their bodies and were utilized for sex by Ba'al's higher-ups.

There were higher level demons who had awakened

inside female humans too. These women were treated differently, garnering the same respect and servility as demon generals.

Tian Gao smiled thinly and turned to snatch the glass of whiskey from the nightstand.

I wonder what sex with one of them would be like. Maybe I'll find out soon.

A ray of sunlight filtered through the drapes across the windows and hit the thin scar on his right wrist.

A wave of anger surged through Tian Gao as he stared at the wound. It was because Yashiro Kuroda's blade had transected his limb so cleanly that doctors had managed to successfully reattach his hand after the incident at the warehouse. The healing abilities of the powerful demon living inside him had taken care of the rest and his arm was nearly as good as new. Tian Gao frowned.

Still, for a human to have bested me is unacceptable.

He was still frowning when someone knocked at the door and walked in without preamble.

"What?" Tian Gao barked at the man hovering on the threshold. "I said I was not to be disturbed, damn it!"

The Triad member glanced at the naked woman on the bed and swallowed convulsively. "I'm sorry, sir, but something urgent has come up."

Tian Gao slammed his whiskey down on the night-stand and shot to his feet. He strode naked across the gloomy bedroom, grabbed the Triad member by the neck, and shoved him up against the wall.

The female demon growled and crawled onto her hands and knees atop the bedsheets, hunger lighting her dark eyes.

"What's so urgent that you had to come in here, huh?!"

Tian Gao snarled, spit flying from his mouth and striking the man he was holding in the face.

The Triad member choked and gurgled, hands clamped around Tian Gao's wrist.

"It's—it's your cousin, sir!" he rasped. "Jiang Fei has gone missing!"

CHAPTER THIRTEEN

"You sure you don't want to come with us?" Artemus said.

Callie shook her head where she bobbed in the water.

"I'm having far too much fun here," she said with a grin, eyeing the men around the hotel swimming pool. "Besides, you guys will be fine for the day, right?"

Artemus looked over at Smokey where the rabbit sat on Callie's towel on a nearby lounge chair. "What about you, Fuzzface?"

Smokey blinked his eyes lazily at him.

"You too, huh?" Artemus said with a faintly accusing frown.

Smokey shuffled around until he had his butt to Artemus.

Artemus sighed. "Fine, be like that."

He headed for the hotel reception, grumbling under his breath all the way.

Elton stood waiting with Drake, Isabelle, Mark, and Shamus. "So, are they coming?"

"No, they're too busy pretending they're on vacation," Artemus snapped.

Isabelle grinned. "I can't say I blame them. L.A. in early spring is quite spectacular."

They left the hotel, climbed into a pair of SUVs with tinted windows, and pulled onto Interstate 10. Artemus watched the sunlit city spread out around them as they crawled through the traffic heading east.

They'd landed in L.A. the previous night, Callie having secured her jet for their private use for the duration of their mission. Although he'd visited the west coast before, it was Artemus's first time in the City of Angels. A wry grimace twisted his lips.

I don't know whether that's irony or a premonition of things to come.

It took them nearly half an hour to navigate the congested roads to Downtown L.A. and the Fashion District, where the demonic manifestations that had attracted the attention of the local Vatican agents had taken place.

They pulled into a multistory carpark close to Santee Alley and stepped out of their vehicles under the watchful gazes of a small group of men and women.

"Isaac," Elton said with a faint smile as he embraced a tall, thin man with a jagged scar on his left jawline. "It's good to see you again, my friend."

"Elton," the man murmured, his stern expression relaxing for a moment. "I didn't know it was you the Vatican was sending to help us out."

Elton made the introductions.

Isaac Seymour, the head of the L.A. Vatican group, studied Artemus with a curious look. "So, you are the infamous Mr. Steele?"

"Who, me?" Artemus shrugged. "I'm just a lowly antique shop owner."

Isaac raised an eyebrow. "Really? I doubt Elton's auction house would be as successful as it is today if it weren't for you." His gaze shifted to Drake. "You, on the other hand, I'm familiar with."

Drake did not reply.

Isaac turned to Elton. "I have to confess to being somewhat puzzled by why you decided to bring a notorious thief and your best antique appraiser along for this. They don't belong here."

"They know about demons," Elton said bluntly. "In fact, they are the prime reason the New York branch of Ba'al no longer exists."

Shocked murmurs broke out among the agents behind Isaac. The man frowned, his eyes full of doubt.

"I read your report to the Vatican about what's been happening in L.A. but these guys," Elton indicated Artemus and Drake, "haven't. So, why don't you tell us the story again."

Isaac wavered for a moment before grabbing a laptop from the SUV behind him and opening it on the hood of the vehicle.

"From what we can make out, the first sighting took place about a month ago. We found mention of a woman's account of what sounded very much like a demon awakening. Local LAPD decided her story was hogwash and shelved it as a hoax call. I had an agent interview her. Her description of what she witnessed happen to her neighbor is pretty undeniable." He opened a 3D map of L.A. and dropped a marker on a location. "We uncovered evidence of five more sightings the same week." He placed more markers on the map. "The week after that, there were ten more."

Unease stirred inside Artemus as he watched the Vatican agent drop more red dots on the screen.

"The penny dropped two weeks ago, when one of our agents read a short news piece about a vicious murder," Isaac continued. "The details were very graphic. But it was a symbol drawn in the victim's blood that caught his attention and made us realize what we were dealing with."

Drake frowned. "Symbol?"

"Yes. An inverted pentagram."

Isabelle narrowed her eyes. "You mean, the Sigil of Baphomet?"

"What's that?" Artemus said, puzzled.

"You really need to brush up on your occult knowledge," Elton muttered. "The Sigil of Baphomet was the official symbol of The Church of Satan, an organization that was disbanded a decade ago." He paused. "Although most people attribute the original concept of the inverted pentagram as a representation of evil to Eliphas Levi, a 19th century French occultist."

Artemus grimaced. "Satan had a church?"

"It wasn't quite a depiction of the sigil, in that it was missing the goat head and the Hebrew letters," Isaac said. "There were other characters at the corners of the pentagram. But we don't know what they mean."

Elton frowned. "Do you have a picture?"

"Sure."

Isaac clicked on a folder and brought up an image.

Artemus startled when he saw the letters Isaac had referred to around the bloodied pentagram.

"That's the same language as in Catherine Boone's journals," Drake muttered.

"Who?" Isaac said.

"I'll explain later," Elton said with a troubled expression. "I take it the Vatican has this image?"

"Yes."

"Let's send it to Otis," Artemus said.

Isaac narrowed his eyes. "Who's Otis?"

"My...assistant."

Guilt flashed through Artemus at the thought of the young man he had left looking after his antique shop in Chicago.

It was after the showdown with Ba'al in New York a few weeks ago that Otis Boone, his assistant of two years, had accidentally become involved in the dark turn that Artemus's life had taken since Smokey had appeared on his doorstep one cold, winter morning. It was Otis who had told Artemus and Callie the names of their weapons and who had led them to his father, William Boone. A man who knew far more about Artemus and Drake's pasts than they knew themselves.

At Otis's family farm outside Pittsburgh, it had become clear to everyone that the young man was more than he seemed too. But what exactly he was no one yet knew. And although he'd said he couldn't decipher his mother's journals, journals which held information about an imminent Judgement Day that would involve Artemus, Drake, Callie, and Smokey among others, Artemus couldn't help but feel that deep inside Otis was a key to unlocking the knowledge Elton and the Vatican sought.

Despite Artemus's effort to pull him out of his shell, the young man had become even more of a recluse since their return from Pittsburgh and refused to engage with anything to do with demons and Ba'al.

"You sure he's gonna want to help?" Drake said, his tone full of doubt.

"We've got nothing to lose by trying," Artemus murmured.

"Where did your agents go missing?" Isabelle asked Isaac.

The Vatican agent turned to the laptop once more. "These are the locations of the last incidents we uncovered, just over two weeks ago. We've had four agents go missing at one of them." His expression hardened. "But it was after reanalyzing the murders last night that we finally grasped a pattern to these demonic sightings."

He placed more markers on the map and zoomed out.

Elton drew a sharp breath. Drake narrowed his eyes.

"Holy shit," Isabelle muttered.

There on the screen, laid out in a garish yet recognizable arrangement of red dots, was an inverted pentagram. And it was centered on Downtown L.A.

A tall, 3D structure stood dead bang in the middle of the design.

Artemus pointed at it. "What is *that?*"

CHAPTER FOURTEEN

"Calm down," Delacourt told the irate man at the other end of the line. "I'm sure your cousin will turn up somewhere." He sighed and rubbed his forehead with his fingers as he listened to Tian Gao's tirade. "No, I didn't mean it like that."

Jesus, this guy's a handful. If it weren't for the fact that he's a demon general, I would have killed him weeks ago.

"Look, I need you to stay put," he told the Triad gang leader. "We want someone powerful close by for when we find it." He paused. "No, I don't know when that will be," he added more sharply than he intended, the demon inside stirring irritably. His smartband buzzed with an incoming message. He narrowed his eyes. "I have to go."

Delacourt ended the call and took a sip of coffee before dialing the number of the person who'd just texted him.

"Hi there," he said coolly. "Long time no hear."

The man at the other end remained silent for a moment.

"They're in L.A.," he finally said.

Delacourt frowned. "Who are in L.A.?"

"Artemus Steele and Drake Hunter."

Delacourt stiffened.

"You guys need to learn to be more subtle," the man continued in a quiet voice. "Those men and that woman you killed a couple of weeks back? The ones who were snooping around? They were Vatican agents. Rome instructed Elton LeBlanc to go to L.A. to assist their local team. He asked Steele and Hunter to go with him."

Delacourt stared over the sunlit city spread out beneath the windows of his highrise office. "Do they know? About what we're after?"

"No," the man replied. "They don't. But they're not stupid. I suggest you speed things up before they find out what's going on."

He ended the call abruptly.

Delacourt listened to the dial tone for a moment before disconnecting. Although he didn't welcome the news he'd just heard, he had to admit to being more than just a little fascinated.

So, I might finally get to meet the infamous Mr. Steele and Mr. Hunter. A faint smile curved his lips as the interest of the demon living under his skin was piqued. *This should be fun.*

～

"This is a bad idea," Ogawa muttered.

"Shut up," Haruki said.

He studied the abandoned hotel a hundred feet up and across the road from where he, Ogawa, and five bodyguards skulked in a narrow side alley in Downtown L.A.

The Art Nouveau building was spread over eight stories, with a curved glass and metal cupola crowning its mansard roof. Despite its tattered facade, it had retained most of its grandeur thanks to a red-brick construct that had stood the test of time, imposing, tall, triple-arched windows, and beautifully designed, whiplash-curved decorative and floral motifs. Haruki stared at the top floor.

That bastard is somewhere up there.

It had taken him several painstaking and bloody hours to extract the information he had wanted from Jiang Fei Hong last night. Of all the Triad members he could have targeted, Haruki had surmised that Tian Gao's cousin would most likely know his whereabouts. And he'd been right.

The knuckles of his right hand prickled where he'd scraped his skin raw. Jiang Fei had withstood his beating for a lot longer than he'd anticipated. Haruki wasn't sure whether it was because the man's senses had been dulled by the alcohol he'd consumed or if it was his duty to his organization that had made him hang on for so long. Jiang Fei had finally revealed Tian Gao's last known location at day break, his battered and bleeding body sagging limply in the chair Haruki had tied him to.

Ogawa had watched on grimly during the interrogation, his disapproval tempered by what Haruki knew was his own burning desire to find the people who'd murdered his brother Riuji.

A shocking surprise had awaited them when they'd looked into the place where Tian Gao had apparently gone into hiding, no doubt ordered to lay low by the head of the L.A. Triad while the latter tried to negotiate with the Kuroda Group to avoid the war looming between them.

The grand hotel, a crumbling relic that had dominated Downtown L.A.'s skyline during the early 20th century, had been purchased by Yashiro Kuroda the week before he went to Hong Kong. Except the deeds and title to the property were now registered to a private organization Haruki had never heard of.

The date of the transfer was the day after Yashiro's murder and the lawyer and county recorder who'd signed off on it were people known to be in the employ of the Triad. Which reinforced Haruki's belief that the documents had been forged.

There was little doubt in Haruki's mind that the hotel he was currently looking at was the piece of prime real estate Sasaki had referred to two nights ago, in Chicago. He narrowed his eyes.

So, this is the place my brother and his men lost their lives over.

From what he and Ogawa had observed thus far, the building was being guarded by a private security firm. Four armed men in dark uniforms bearing a logo they didn't recognize stood in front of the main doors. They'd spotted as many at the rear of the building.

Haruki slipped his smart glasses on and swiped through the floorplans he'd scanned an hour ago. He brought up a map he'd downloaded from the City of Los Angeles's open data portal, examined the complex lines crisscrossing this part of downtown, and finally found what he was looking for.

"We're gonna need a sledgehammer," he told Ogawa grimly.

～

"ARE YOU PROPOSING WE JUST WALTZ IN THERE?"

Artemus met Isaac's cynical stare in the rearview mirror of the SUV before gazing at the building down the road.

He sensed faint demonic energy coming from the structure they'd been watching for the last half hour and could see the dark tendrils of corruption swirling above the heads of the uniformed men guarding its entrance, even from this distance.

There was something else. Something vaguely familiar he'd picked up on when they first arrived at their current location. Artemus frowned. Whatever it was, he couldn't feel it anymore.

A black van pulled up in front of the building.

A group of men came out of the front doors and headed toward it. Two of them were carrying boxes. The others maneuvered a marble fireplace across the sidewalk and into the back of the vehicle.

Artemus and the others stared at the van when it drove past them a moment later.

"What was that about?" Drake muttered.

"Did you see the logo on the side?" Artemus said pensively.

"Yeah." Elton grimaced. "Not exactly subtle, are they?"

The name "Leviathan" had been etched in white on the van's side panel. Beneath it had been a graphic of the legendary beast in vivid orange.

"All this sitting around is getting us nowhere," Artemus said with a sigh. "Why don't I go check out the place? See if they'll let me take a look inside."

Everyone stared at him.

"Are you crazy?" Drake said with a scowl.

"Look, we just lost some of our best agents in that place," Isaac said stiffly. "I really don't think—"

Artemus stepped out of the SUV.

"See you in five," he said breezily before slamming the door shut on a barrage of shocked faces.

He headed into a shop, came out with a paper map, and strode confidently toward the building that formed the center of the demonic pentagram Isaac and his agents had recently deciphered.

One of the guards spotted him when he was still fifty feet away and watched him approach with a stony stare.

"Hey." Artemus stopped and flashed them a friendly smile. "I hear this is a must-see tourist spot downtown." He showed them the map he was holding. "Can I take a look inside?"

The men glanced at each other, as if not quite believing their ears.

Artemus took a step toward the doors. The guards straightened and blocked his path, their hands on the butts of the guns in their hip holsters.

"Whoa there," Artemus murmured.

He kept his expression neutral as the men's foul auras visibly thickened.

"This building is off limits, asshole," one of the guards growled. "So, why don't you fuck the hell off?"

Artemus put a hand up in a placatory gesture. "Alright. I didn't mean any harm."

He turned and headed down the road, conscious of the men's eyes on his back. The SUV was waiting for him around the corner.

"Please abstain from doing stupid things like that in the future," Elton said darkly as he climbed into the back. "I just aged ten years."

"Well?" Drake asked impatiently.

"We need to find a way into that building," Artemus said in a hard voice. "There must be a damn good reason why there's an army of demons guarding the place."

CHAPTER FIFTEEN

HARUKI WIPED SWEAT-STREAKED DIRT FROM HIS FACE, stepped over the pile of broken bricks at his feet, and climbed through the gaping hole in the wall.

"Be careful," Ogawa murmured.

The bodyguard followed closely behind Haruki with the rest of their men.

Haruki paused in the darkness and switched on his flashlight.

The cavernous basement of the hotel came into view in the beam of bright light. Judging from the rotting card-board boxes and damaged furniture crowding the floor, and the rank smell of mold and the staleness saturating the air, no one had been down there for a while.

It was the sewer map he'd downloaded from the city's online portal that had provided Haruki with a way inside the building. He'd figured whoever was in charge of guarding the hotel was unlikely to have posted men in the basement since they would not be expecting a break-in from below. So far, it looked like he'd been right.

He made his way carefully through the low-ceiling

chamber and came to a metal door on the other side. It was locked.

One of their men used a pick lock to open it. They twisted suppressors on the ends of their guns and silently climbed the flight of steps on the other side. A gloomy passage appeared at the top. Haruki put his smart glasses on and brought up the building floorplans.

They were in a service corridor at the back of the hotel.

"This way," he murmured and turned left.

They came to another door some thirty feet later.

Haruki's pulse accelerated as he reached for the knob and slowly twisted it. The hinges creaked when he started to push the door open. He froze, conscious of the tense men at his back. They stood still for a moment.

No sound came from the interior of the hotel.

Haruki opened the door ever so slowly. A murky space materialized before him.

It was the rear lobby of the hotel.

He stepped out into it and glimpsed the shadowy shapes of the guards stationed at the back of the building through the frosted glass doors on his right.

Haruki indicated a metal curtain pole lying on the floor nearby. Two of his men lifted it and quietly slipped the rod through the handles of the back doors.

That should hold them off for some time.

He headed left with Ogawa and the other bodyguards.

They navigated a deserted hallway with marble floors and peeling floral wallpaper, passed two grand reception rooms and a dining room that could easily seat several hundred guests, and finally reached a large lobby at the front of the building. Haruki took his smart glasses off and studied the imposing space around them.

From its mosaic flooring and the decorative stucco gracing its walls to its elaborate, coffered ceiling with its crystal chandeliers, the hotel's main reception had weathered the passage of time better than the rest of the building so far.

I can see why Yashiro was keen on this place. It has huge potential.

Haruki's gaze zeroed in on the wide, split-level, wrought-iron staircase that took center stage in the middle of the foyer. He moved determinedly toward it.

"Master Haruki, wait!" Ogawa hissed.

Voices reached Haruki's ears. A door opened on their left. Three men walked out of what looked like a back office. They paused mid-conversation and froze in their tracks, surprise widening their eyes.

Haruki knew they were Triad members from the tattoos peeking out from the neckline of their shirts. He raised his gun and fired at them at the same time as Ogawa and the other bodyguards.

The men jerked and stumbled back as their bullets slammed into them.

The hairs rose on Haruki's nape.

"What the hell?" Ogawa murmured in a shocked voice.

The Triad members were still standing. They looked slowly from the bullet holes peppering their bodies to the group who'd just shot at them. Their lips curved into sadistic smiles. One of them touched the black liquid oozing out of the wound in his abdomen and licked his finger, his expression growing hungry.

Thump.

Haruki startled.

The men's eyes darkened, the whites turning pure

obsidian. Their pupils changed next and became glowing, yellow centers filled with evil.

"Oh God," one of Haruki's bodyguards mumbled, his face ashen. "They are—"

"Demons!" Ogawa spat out.

Thump-thump.

Haruki raised a trembling hand to his chest as a heavy, suffocating feeling filled his lungs.

Thump-thump. Thump-thump.

A lightheaded sensation washed over him. He swayed where he stood, stunned by the heartbeat resonating violently against his ribs.

It did not belong to him.

Ogawa's voice reached him dimly through the ringing in his ears. "Master Haruki?"

What is this? What's happening to me?

Ogawa grabbed his shoulder and yanked him toward the hallway they'd come from. "We have to leave. *Now!*"

Haruki shuddered.

Too late.

The Triad members moved, their bodies morphing as they crossed the distance separating them from Haruki and his bodyguards in leaps and bounds. Their chests swelled. Their limbs thickened. Their hands and feet extended and curved into deadly talons. Their faces twisted until they resembled creatures that did not belong to this world.

Haruki's stomach lurched as time slowed. It was in that moment he finally acknowledged to himself that he had not truly believed Sasaki's fantastical account of what had happened on the day Yashiro was murdered. Nor had he been convinced by what Artemus had told him about the supposed demonic organization he and his companions had crossed paths with in Chicago and New York.

They were right. They were right, all along. And we're going to die, here, today, because I refused to trust them!

Something shifted deep inside Haruki then, as if in response to the words he'd just silently screamed internally. Goosebumps exploded across his body. His skin quivered. His flesh tingled. His blood fluttered. His bones shook.

Thump-thump. Thump-thump. Thump-thump.

A shudder raced through him from the top of his head to the tips of his toes. Something was coming. Rising from the very depths of his soul. Something powerful. Something terrifying.

Heat erupted inside his body, a conflagration that made him gasp at the same time that it filled him with the most incredible feeling of potency.

Haruki stepped instinctively in front of his men and raised his right hand. Crimson light flashed on his juzu bracelet. It transformed into a flaming sword with a gilded hilt.

He blinked as the blade impaled the demon springing toward him.

CHAPTER SIXTEEN

"WHOSE IDEA WAS THIS AGAIN?" DRAKE SAID. "OH, yeah. Yours."

He gave Artemus a dirty look.

"My clothes are going to stink for the rest of the day," Isabelle said morosely. "No. Make that the rest of the week."

"I can barely smell anything anymore," Mark said with a pained expression. "My olfactory nerves shut down two blocks ago."

"I hear you," Shamus muttered. "You could blindfold me and wave a dead skunk in front of me right now and I wouldn't be able to tell."

"Will you guys stop bitching?" Artemus snapped.

He raised his flashlight. The light beam pierced the gloom of the dank sewer they were navigating.

"We must be close," Elton mumbled from behind the handkerchief he was holding over his mouth.

"It should be around the next corner," Isaac said.

They reached a junction and turned left. Rats scuttled past them as they advanced along the gloomy conduit.

Something shadowy rose on the path ahead some thirty feet later. Artemus slowed.

His breath caught when he saw what appeared in the pale glow of his light. "Someone got here before us."

He stopped in front of a pile of rubble and stared at the gaping hole in the wall above it.

"How do you know?" one of Isaac's agents said in a doubtful tone. "This could have been here from a while back."

"The brick dust is fresh," Artemus replied quietly. "So are those footprints."

The agent stared at the imprints on the ground.

Artemus climbed through the opening and shone his light around the basement of the abandoned hotel while the others joined him.

"Well, at least it's better than the sewers," Isabelle muttered, wrinkling her nose at the musty smell.

Artemus started across the chamber and was halfway to the other side when the hairs suddenly rose on his arms. He stopped dead in his tracks.

"Artemus," Drake said in a low voice.

Artemus frowned. "Yeah, I feel it."

Warmth suffused his body from the wing marks on his back as he sensed the waves of demonic energy roiling through the building. It was stronger than it had been outside. And it was growing, rapidly.

There was something else. An echo of power that seemed vaguely familiar. It was the same thing he thought he'd sensed when they'd first arrived at the building that morning.

It kinda resembles Callie and Smo—

Artemus scowled when he finally recognized the life force he'd just detected. "That dumbass!"

"What is it?" Elton asked stiffly.

Artemus reached for the switchblade in his boot and unleashed the sword within.

Isaac drew a sharp breath. "What the—?"

Drake's watch morphed into a metal shield that covered his left arm at the same time that the knife he'd pulled out of the sheath at his waist transformed into a sword.

"Is that who I think it is?" he said with a grimace.

"Yeah," Artemus said grimly. "Let's go!"

He headed rapidly for the half-open door on the other side of the basement.

HARUKI GASPED AND JUMPED OUT OF THE WAY OF A SET of wicked talons. The tips grazed his abdomen fleetingly. He blocked the next strike with the fiery sword in his hands, kicked the demon coming at him from the right in the stomach, and beheaded the creature in front of him.

The demon thudded to the ground, his body resuming its normal human appearance once more in death.

Ogawa swore where he stood a few feet to Haruki's left. He glanced from the blood oozing out of the fresh slashes in his left forearm to the demon who'd clawed him. He ducked beneath the savage fist coming at his face and stabbed the creature straight through the eye as he rose. The demon shrieked and stumbled backward.

Haruki glanced at the bodyguards behind them, his heart hammering against his ribs. Two of them were down, unconscious but alive. The other three were on their hands and knees, blood dripping from their various wounds and their chests heaving from the unnatural battle that had been unleashed upon them several minutes earlier.

Although Haruki had successfully felled the first three creatures who had attacked them, more had appeared, drawn by the sounds of the battle. He turned and faced the dark figures emerging from the depths of the hotel, his knuckles whitening on the handle of his blade.

He did not understand how his bracelet had transformed into a sword, nor why he could wield the weapon as if it were an extension of his body. And he could not put a name to the glorious energy pouring through his limbs from the depths of his soul, or the being he could sense lurking behind his eyes.

No. Not being. Haruki frowned. *Beast.*

There was only one thing he was certain of right now.

He had been born to use this sword.

"Ogawa, take our men and leave," Haruki said in a hard voice as the demons surrounded them.

"What?" the bodyguard barked. "Are you crazy?!"

"No, I'm not. I'm the one they're after."

Haruki moved across the lobby to prove his point. The demons followed him with their gazes, their heads pivoting smoothly as if they were a single creature.

"Go," he ordered. "*Now!* While I have their attention!"

"No," Ogawa said between gritted teeth.

Haruki scowled. "You're such a stubborn bas—"

He froze, the rest of the words dying on his lips.

Ogawa followed his gaze up the staircase.

Tian Gao stood watching them from the second-floor balcony, a horde of demons at his side. Recognition dawned on his pockmarked face.

A scornful smile twisted his lips. "Well, if it isn't little

Haruki Kuroda and his minions. I was wondering who was causing such a ruckus."

Haruki's eyes widened as the man vaulted smoothly over the balustrade and dropped some thirty feet onto the lobby floor. He stumbled when the mosaic floor shook and cracked under the impact of the Triad gang leader's landing.

By the time Tian Gao rose to his full height, he was no longer human.

"Was it you who took Jiang Fei?" the demon growled.

Haruki swallowed as he gazed at the giant creature towering over him.

Shit. He's much bigger than the others.

"Answer me, you little rat!" Tian Gao roared.

A fist slammed into Haruki's solar plexus and lifted him off his feet. He gasped, stars flashing in front of his eyes and his breath locking in his throat as pain exploded inside him. He struck the wall next to the front doors hard and slid down limply onto sagging knees, air wheezing out of his lips.

Haruki coughed up a mouthful of blood and raised his head in time to see Tian Gao charge at him, the demon's colossal body blurring with the speed of his attack. He pushed away from the wall and clasped his sword in a double-handed grip, his pulse hammering away in his veins.

I can't dodge this!

The Triad gang leader skidded to an abrupt stop five feet from him. Haruki blinked.

Someone had just stepped in the demon's path.

"Hi there. Look, would you mind terribly pretending this never happened? My young friend here is being an ass, so I would appreciate it if you could let him go, just this once."

Haruki stared from Artemus to the sword the blond man was holding in his right hand. The blade shimmered with a white haze, as if it were lit from within. It looked bigger than when he'd first seen it two days ago, in the man's kitchen in Chicago.

Tian Gao gazed at the tip of the sword where it had stopped a mere inch from piercing his heart. He raised his head and studied the armed group who'd appeared from the rear of the hotel with narrowed eyes.

The only other person Haruki recognized was Drake. And the man looked different from the last time he'd seen him too. For one thing, his eyes were glowing with a red light. And in his right hand was a blade as different from Artemus's as light was from day. It was made of a dark metal, its edges wicked, serrated teeth designed to shred an enemy to pieces.

Haruki glanced at the shield covering Drake's left arm, before focusing on the man who'd probably just saved him from being killed.

"Who the fuck are you?" Tian Gao asked Artemus darkly.

Artemus scratched his nose, his expression still relaxed. "I'd love to give you my business card, but I forgot to bring one."

Tian Gao snarled and grabbed at Artemus's sword. The blond man whipped a gun out from his back and fired at the demon, his movement as fast as the giant creature's.

Tian Gao let go of the blade and stumbled back a step. He gazed at the shallow crater in his abdomen, surprise widening his obsidian eyes. Faint, orange cracks appeared at the edges of the wound.

"That was a silver-leaded bullet impregnated with Holy Water," Artemus said in a conversational voice.

Haruki stared at the weapon in Artemus's hand. He'd never seen a firearm like it before.

"It would have killed a normal demon," Artemus continued in the same light tone. "Like, poof. Sudden glowing fiend, burst of flames, cloud of ash. Alas, it only seems to hurt big bastards like you."

Haruki stiffened when the air thickened with a foul energy. An eerie twilight fell across the lobby. Artemus straightened, his expression sobering as he watched the creatures around them gather for an attack.

Tian Gao and the other demons suddenly froze. They cocked their heads to the west, as if listening to a voice no one else could hear. Drake startled.

Artemus looked over at him, a faint frown marring his brow.

Tian Gao gnashed his teeth.

"Retreat!" he growled, his voice full of frustration.

The demons stepped into the shadows and soon faded to swirling wisps of darkness. A deathly silence descended on the hotel lobby.

"Alright," Isaac said grimly. "Will someone explain to me what the hell just happened here?"

Elton studied Haruki and the flaming sword with a frown.

"Who is he?" he asked Artemus.

CHAPTER SEVENTEEN

DELACOURT DIPPED HIS CHIN AT HIS STAFF AS HE strolled through the building and headed out to the pool area. He navigated the sun-drenched patio and the dozen guests on lounge chairs before stopping where a beautiful woman in a sundress lay with her eyes closed behind her sunglasses.

"I hope the hotel is to your liking, Mrs. Stone," he drawled.

Callie Stone blinked. She sat up slowly and tipped the glasses up onto her head.

"Hello," she said with a quizzical smile. "Yes, it is."

"Forgive my audacity, but once I discovered the widow of Ronald Stone was staying with us, I decided to move you and your companions to the Presidential Suite," Delacourt said. "I mean Mr. Steele and Mr. Hunter. I wouldn't have it otherwise."

He glanced at the rabbit crouched by the blonde's feet. The creature stared back at him with intelligent brown eyes.

"Oh, you shouldn't have," Callie protested. "Are you the owner of the hotel?"

"Yes, I am. Daniel Delacourt, at your service." He smiled. "Would you do me the honor of having lunch with me? I can have it served in your new suite, if that would make you more comfortable."

Callie observed him for a moment, her green eyes unreadable. "Sure."

She picked up her carryall and the silver-and-gold-plated ivory cane propped against her chair before following him into the hotel, the rabbit at her side.

"What's his name?" Delacourt said as they entered an elevator.

"Smokey," Callie replied.

They rode up to the tenth floor, negotiated the north corridor, and finally arrived at the Presidential Suite. Callie's eyes widened with appreciation when she stepped inside. She observed the expensively furnished, open-plan lounge-dining room around her before crossing the floor to a glass wall that looked out onto a private patio with an uninterrupted vista of Beverly Hills.

"Now, that's what you call a view."

"I'm glad you like it," Delacourt murmured.

A knock came at the door. The maître d'hôtel walked in with a trolley bearing several silver cloche serving dishes and a bottle of red wine.

They followed him to the dining table.

"We have artichoke soup for starter, sauté de boeuf with cream and mushroom sauce as the main course, and strawberry cheesecake for dessert," the maître d'hôtel said, uncovering their food. "I hope everything is to your liking."

"I'm sure it will be," Callie said, eyeing it all with a

delighted expression. She glanced at Smokey. "I see you even brought something for my friend."

The rabbit's eyes had glazed over slightly at the delicious aromas filling the suite. He stared unblinkingly at the dish Callie placed on the floor in front of him and let out a huff of appreciation.

Delacourt chuckled. "He's a delightful little thing, isn't he?"

They chatted about Callie's late husband's business ventures and world politics over their meal. To his surprise, Delacourt found himself enjoying the blonde's company. Although she initially came across as an airhead, Callie Stone was bright and sharp-witted.

They had finished their main course and were on dessert and coffee when he sat back in his chair and studied her with a pensive expression.

"Is everything okay?" Callie asked with a puzzled half-smile.

"Yes, it is," Delacourt replied. "I find myself strangely comfortable in your company. I wonder if it's because of what you are."

≈

CALLIE FROZE. SHE PUT HER FORK DOWN CAREFULLY, wiped her lips with a napkin, and stared at the handsome, blond, brown-eyed man across the table from her.

It had taken her a moment, down by the pool, to sense that something wasn't quite right with Daniel Delacourt. What it was though, she still wasn't sure. Even Smokey seemed puzzled by the man.

His aura was hard to read.

"And what do you mean by that, exactly?" she said in a mild tone.

Delacourt raised an eyebrow. "Why, a monster, of course."

Callie's ears popped as the pressure inside the room dropped. Thin coils of darkness materialized out of the air and filled the room with a suffocating feeling of corruption. Her pulse spiked.

Demon!

She snatched the cane from where it rested against the table leg next to her and jumped out of the chair at the same time that Smokey exploded into his hellhound form. Bright lines flashed across the shaft of the walking stick, forming holy sigils that only Callie could translate. It transformed into a golden scepter the next instant.

Callie's hair thickened and lengthened into hundreds of flaxen-colored snakes. Her nails extended into vicious claws. Her tailbone itched and grew a serpent as thick as her arm and nearly as tall as herself. And on her forehead, ivory stubs sprouted into wickedly curved horns designed to maim and gore.

Delacourt blinked, his expression unfazed. He rose to his feet and slowly clapped his hands.

"Bravo," he said in a heartfelt voice. "What an incredible show! Without a doubt, you must be the most beautiful of all the divine beasts, Chimera."

Surprise jolted through Callie.

Divine what?

Delacourt's gaze shifted to Smokey. The hellhound's eyes glowed a savage red as he glared at the man on the other side of the table, his lips peeling back to reveal his deadly fangs.

"You are also a most splendid animal, my dear Cerberus, even though you are not in your full form."

"How do you know who we are?" Callie asked, smoke curling around her mouth from the fiery power churning inside her belly. "And how did you do that?"

Delacourt smiled.

"Do what, my dear?" he said, ignoring her first question.

Callie narrowed her eyes at his condescending tone.

"Hide your aura like that," she snapped. "I couldn't sense it until now."

Delacourt rubbed his chin pensively and slowly walked around the table. "Well, you see, there are many levels of demons."

Callie's heart thudded rapidly as the air trembled with a raw, brutal energy.

He was still masking his power?!

"You have your low-level ones, creatures who are slaves to their base instincts and who kill for no reason but the pure joy of it," Delacourt continued, oblivious to Callie's shock. "They form the, how should I put it—" a wry expression dawned on his face, "crux of our army. Then, there are demons that humans would consider lieutenants and captains. They are more intelligent and are able to control the lower level demons. Finally, we have the high-level demons. *They* are the most valuable members of our race. And of those there are two subclasses." He paused, his voice still calm. "Generals, like Jade Q. And commanders, like Erik Park. Both of whom you and your friends killed in New York." He shrugged. "Erik had always been a bit of a hothead. Commanders can usually mask their auras but he chose not to, most of the time."

"Stop right there!" Callie growled. "Come any closer and I will kill you!"

Flames burst into life on the tips of her horns. Smokey's body grew another foot and his eyes went from red to gold as his power increased.

Delacourt halted in his tracks.

"There is no need to defend yourselves," he said quietly. "I am only here to make you an offer."

Callie blinked when the dark forces pervading the suite suddenly abated, as if a switch had been flicked off.

"Join us," Delacourt said. "With the two of you at our side, our army will be a force to be reckoned with."

Callie stared, too shocked to speak for a moment.

"What on earth makes you think we would accept your offer and betray our friends?" she finally said.

Delacourt smiled thinly. "Because we will be victorious. However much the Vatican and their allies try to stop us, nothing can allay what is coming."

Callie scowled. "And what's that?"

"Why, Judgement Day, of course," Delacourt said, matter-of-factly. He paused. "Our Master felt that if we were to cross paths with you again, we should offer you divine beasts the chance to be on the winning side of that battle."

Smokey growled, anger roiling off him in thick waves.

"Why do you keep calling us that?" Callie asked.

Genuine surprise flashed across Delacourt's handsome face. He stared at them for a stunned moment before bursting into laughter.

"Oh my!" he gasped between chortles, bending over and clasping his midriff, "don't tell me you don't even know what you truly are?!"

Callie glared at him while he slowly sobered and wiped tears of merriment from his face.

"How pitiful," Delacourt said once he could speak again. "If this is the extent of knowledge your army possesses, then we *will* be victorious."

A knock came at the door of the suite. Someone tried the handle and walked in.

"Hey, guys?" Serena said. "Reception said you'd been upgraded to the Presidential—"

She froze when she saw them. Nate came to a stop behind her, his face growing focused as he registered Callie and Smokey in their beast forms.

Delacourt studied the newcomers with a curious look. "Ah. The super soldiers." He smiled. "Interesting."

Serena frowned at the blond man. Her gaze shifted to Callie and Smokey.

"Is everything okay?" she asked in a steely voice.

Callie hesitated before nodding. She shifted back to her human appearance, her right hand still locked solidly around the scepter. She could sense no threat from Delacourt.

Not right now, anyway.

Smokey stayed in his hellhound form, his eyes full of wariness still.

"Well, it's been a pleasant meeting," Delacourt said lightly. He bowed his head at Callie. "Thank you for a most enlightening meal." He paused, his smile widening. "Your other friends should be here soon. It seems they got into some trouble downtown."

Callie stiffened. Delacourt waved his hand in a general goodbye and strolled out of the suite. The sound of the door closing behind him echoed in the taut silence.

"What was that about?" Serena said.

CHAPTER EIGHTEEN

"WE'RE LEAVING," CALLIE SAID.

Artemus slowed to a stop inside the hotel lobby, Drake and Elton at his side. He stared from Callie and Smokey's stiff expressions to Serena and Nate.

"What's going on?" he asked. "And what's with all the luggage?"

He indicated the cases and bags piled on the floor behind them.

"I'll explain in the car," Callie said grimly. "We need to get out of this place. Right now!"

She grabbed her stuff and headed determinedly outside, Smokey hopping beside her.

"What's happening?" Elton said, bewildered.

"Hell if I know," Drake muttered, staring in the direction in which Callie and Smokey had disappeared.

"What are you two doing here?" Artemus asked Serena and Nate.

"Lou and Tom are back in the country. They took Sasaki off us last night," Serena replied. "We thought we'd take Elton up on his offer since we had some free time." She shrugged her backpack on her shoulder. "Let's go."

Callie was sitting in the one of the SUVs with Smokey when they reached the car park. Isabelle, Mark, and Shamus stood outside the vehicle and stared at her with puzzled expressions.

"She said we're leaving?" Isabelle asked Elton quizzically.

"Nate and I walked in on Callie in Chimera form when we got to the hotel a short while ago," Serena said, her expression cautious as she gazed at the scowling woman inside the SUV. "Smokey was in his hellhound shape too."

Artemus startled.

"There was a guy there. Someone we didn't recognize," Nate added grimly. "Whatever he said to Callie and Smokey seems to have pissed them off big time." He paused. "And he knew Serena and I were super soldiers."

Artemus frowned. "What?"

He turned and studied Callie and Smokey through the window. He could feel the anger echoing through the hellhound across the bond that linked them and knew Drake felt it too. And he had never seen Callie like this before. Gone was the lighthearted and carefree woman he was used to. This Callie was serious as shit and looked ready to kick someone's ass.

"What do you want to do?" Elton said, frowning.

"If Callie says we should leave, then we go," Artemus said.

Nate took the wheel of their SUV while Elton and his team headed for the second vehicle.

It wasn't until they hit Santa Monica Boulevard and turned north toward Holmby Hills under Callie's instructions that she finally related what had happened back at the hotel.

Tension wound through Artemus as he listened to her.

"He knew what had happened downtown?" he said quietly when she finished.

"Yes."

Damn. Was this Delacourt guy the one who called off Tian Gao Lee and the other demons just before they were going to attack us?

Artemus exchanged a troubled glance with Drake. The look in his brother's eyes told him he was thinking the same thing. Artemus frowned faintly. There was something he hadn't asked Drake yet. Something that disturbed him as much as Callie's account.

There had been a moment, back at the abandoned hotel downtown, when Drake had looked surprised, just before Tian Gao and the other demons disappeared. Artemus was willing to bet a lot of money that his brother had heard the demonic call too.

Callie gnawed on her bottom lip and glanced at the mansions rolling past the window. "He said there were several levels of demons. The higher level ones, like that Jade Q woman Serena killed in New York, are generals. Above them are commanders, like Park and Delacourt." She hesitated. "Commanders can mask their demonic auras." Her eyes darkened with disquiet. "Although I could tell something wasn't quite right with the man, I didn't sense the extent of his powers until he allowed me to. And neither did Smokey."

Her fingers clenched on Smokey's fur where he sat on her lap. The rabbit turned and headbutted her hands gently.

Artemus stared at Smokey. "Is that why you decided to stay with Callie this morning?"

Smokey huffed.

That whole place felt strange. But, like my sister, I could not sense the reason why until that man chose to reveal his powers.

"Delacourt called us divine beasts," Callie said. "He knows more about us than we know ourselves, Artemus. That's what upsets me the most about all of this. He said —he said that Ba'al would win because we don't know what we truly are!"

Artemus did not reply. That fact bothered him too. Because he could sense the truth in it. Right now, they were flailing in the dark. Everything that had happened since that night in Chicago when they first met. Everything that they had done since then. All of it felt as if they were being swept away by circumstances beyond their control. Like hapless victims in a game of chess, or marionettes being controlled by an unseen puppeteer.

There's a bigger picture here that we are yet to see. And I think we'll find some of the answers we seek in Catherine Boone's journals.

"We're here," Callie murmured.

Nate slowed to a stop in front of a gated property at the end of a cul-de-sac. Callie leaned out of the SUV's window and input an access code into the security panel on the post next to the road. The barriers opened ponderously to reveal a paved, winding driveway. They rolled onto it and pulled into the courtyard of a large, Spanish-style mansion moments later.

Artemus eyed the split-level building set amidst beautifully landscaped gardens. "Whose place is this?"

"Friends of mine," Callie replied. "They're on vacation in Europe right now. I asked if we could use their home as our base of operations." She stepped out of the SUV and greeted the housekeeper who came out of the front doors with a weak smile. "Hi, Elena. Thank you for having us on such short notice."

"The pleasure is all mine, Mrs. Stone," the middle-aged woman said graciously. "There are refreshments in the main lounge. If you would care to go there, I shall get your rooms ready."

"Why didn't we come here in the first place?" Drake muttered as the housekeeper disappeared.

Callie hesitated. "I did think about it. Then I remembered the state of the mansion in Chicago." She sniffed. "You and Serena can be right slobs. At least Artemus and Nate pick up after themselves."

"Hey!" Serena protested with a scowl.

CHAPTER NINETEEN

"So, what exactly happened downtown?"

Drake grimaced at Serena's question. "It was a disaster."

They'd gathered in a large, open-plan, living-dining room at the rear of the mansion. It looked out onto the back garden and an infinity pool with views over the Los Angeles basin.

Surprise dawned on Serena, Nate, and Callie's faces as Drake and Artemus filled them in on what they'd learned from Isaac and his team that morning, and what they'd found at the abandoned hotel that formed the epicenter of the inverted pentagram the demon sightings had formed over Downtown L.A.

"So, the Yakuza kid's bracelet transformed?" Nate murmured.

"Yeah." Isabelle made a face. "I gotta say, I've seen plenty of wild things in my lifetimes, but that flaming sword of his sure was a humdinger." She cocked her head at Artemus and Drake. "A bit like theirs."

"You never said you'd met Haruki Kuroda in Chicago,"

Elton told Artemus accusingly. "Or what happened with that bracelet of his when he broke into your place."

Drake and Artemus had told Elton about their first encounter with Haruki after they had left the hotel downtown.

"Yeah, well, I had other stuff on my mind," Artemus muttered. "Like someone asking me to come to L.A. to chase demons."

Callie's fingers clenched around the cup of coffee in her hand as she gazed at Artemus and Drake. "Haruki *is* really one of us then, isn't he?"

Artemus hesitated. "I think so. His energy signature is similar to yours and Smokey's. But I don't know what exactly he is, yet."

Serena frowned at Drake. "Did you ask him about marks? You know, like the wings you and Artemus have on your backs, and the symbols Callie has on her body?"

"We didn't get to," Drake replied in a disgusted tone. "That ungrateful little shit hightailed out of there the minute we got outside the building."

"To be fair, I think he was still shellshocked," Artemus said.

"Don't go defending the brat," Drake retorted. "You said it yourself. He was a dumbass for thinking he could go up against an entire horde of demons."

He was still unnerved about what had happened back at the abandoned hotel. Like before, the presence of demons had stirred the one living inside him. His very own private demon. The devil he'd spent most of his life trying to hold back. And that hadn't been the worst of it. No, the worst thing had happened at the very end of their encounter with Tian Gao and his demonic cronies.

Drake's stomach twisted as he recalled the voice he'd

heard inside his head. The one that had reached him as clearly as if the other person had been standing in that hotel lobby with them. For a moment, Drake had felt the dark pull that had drawn Tian Gao and the other demons into the shadows. And, for a second, his body had almost moved against his own volition to try and follow them.

Drake stared into his coffee.

There were two things that had stopped him in his tracks.

One was his bond with Artemus. A bond his brother had unconsciously switched up by another degree in that very instant, as if he'd feared he would lose Drake to the other side. He scowled.

The second was the fact that he was damned if he'd let the demon inside him win after so long.

I've held that bastard back for over twenty years. I can hold him back for another twenty.

As if to tease him, the demon laughed faintly in the back of his mind.

Elton's voice distracted him from his grim thoughts. "Isaac said he'd call when he had further news about that hotel."

"Do you know why they were there?" Artemus asked the older man curiously. "Apart from the fact that it was the focal point of that pentagram. I mean, we didn't find anything notable in the quick search we did of the place after they left. Was it just some kind of demon den?"

"They were looking for something," Drake said.

Artemus looked at him, clearly puzzled.

"Remember the stuff they took away in that van?" Drake reminded him. "There were faded marks on the floors and walls of that hotel. I bet there were objects there that have been moved recently."

Elton glanced at Shamus, Isabelle, and Mark with a guarded expression.

Artemus narrowed his eyes at his friend and mentor. "There's something you're not telling us, isn't there?"

Elton hesitated.

"Spill it," Artemus ordered in a stony voice, "or we'll be on Callie's jet in the next hour, making our merry way back to Chicago."

"Alright. But this information is for your ears only, understood?" Elton said stiffly.

"It's not as if anyone else would believe this stuff even if we told them," Serena murmured.

"From the findings of the experts who've been examining the arch we found in the cave in New York, the Vatican believes the artifact was discovered in Jerusalem some two decades ago," Elton said. "They sent a team to Israel recently to look into any unusual events that may have transpired in the city around that time. The investigation came up with some interesting findings." He paused, lines furrowing his brow. "It appears as if there was a local rise in demonic manifestations just before Ba'al found the gate."

"Are you saying the demons were—what, *attracted* to the gate? And that's how Ba'al found it?" Artemus said skeptically.

"That doesn't make sense," Drake told Elton. "Chances are that thing had been there for hundreds, if not thousands, of years. Why then?"

"Did you say the gate was discovered by Ba'al around twenty years ago?" Callie mumbled.

Drake stared at her. The color had drained from the blonde's face.

Artemus drew a sharp breath, understanding dawning in his eyes. "Damn. The cane!"

His gaze shifted to the ivory walking stick propped against Callie's chair.

"What is it?" Elton said.

Callie picked up the artifact.

"Ronald bought this in Jerusalem, twenty years ago," she said in a stunned voice as she stared at the walking stick. She looked up at them, her expression glazed. "He found it in a shop in the Old City."

There was a shocked silence.

"Holy crumbs," Isabelle said in an awed voice.

"If the cane was the key to the gate and they were discovered close to one another—" Artemus started, his expression growing grim.

"And one or the other was what caused a sudden rise in demon awakening—" Serena said, her eyes narrowing.

"Then what's happening in L.A. right now could be a repeat of Jerusalem," Drake finished, the same fear igniting inside him.

"There might be another gate in that abandoned hotel downtown?" Callie stared at Elton, obviously shaken. "Is that what you're saying?"

"Yes," Elton replied in a troubled voice. "That's what the Vatican thinks."

"Jesus, how many of those things are there?" Drake muttered.

"We don't know," Elton said. "And it *is* just a theory at the moment."

"I think your theory might be correct," Artemus said darkly.

Nate frowned. "Aren't you guys forgetting something?"

They stared at him.

"Didn't Haruki mention that his brother brought that bracelet of his back from Hong Kong about a month ago?" Nate continued. "Like, around the time you said the demonic manifestations in L.A. started?"

Artemus paled. "Shit."

CHAPTER TWENTY

"I THOUGHT I MADE IT CRYSTAL CLEAR THAT YOU WERE to stay away from the Triad," Akihito Kuroda said icily.

Haruki's fingers curled into fists at his sides, his head still spinning in the wake of everything that had happened an hour past.

After Artemus had rescued him and his men from the demons, Haruki had left the hotel hastily, eager to put as much distance between himself and that cursed place as he possibly could. There had also been his wounded body-guards to contend with.

Ogawa had called ahead before they reached the Kuroda estate to request the assistance of the private doctors who usually attended to the medical needs of the members of their organization. To Haruki's surprise, his father had been waiting for them on the doorstep of the mansion when they arrived.

Akihito Kuroda's arctic gaze shifted to the man standing beside Haruki. "I am disappointed in you, Renji. I specifically asked you to stop my stupid son from doing anything that would jeopardize my current talks with the head of the Triad. If it weren't for the recent death of your brother, I would be asking for a finger right now."

A muscle jumped in Ogawa's cheek at the mention of the punitive Yakuza ritual. "I'm sorry, boss."

"Renji did nothing wrong," Haruki protested. "And I know Tian Gao Lee's location. He was—"

His father closed the gap between them and slapped him across the face.

Haruki's head twisted sharply to the side with the force of the blow. He touched a thumb to his split lower lip and stared at the blood on his fingertip before gazing at the man before him, his heart pounding.

In all his years, his father had never once laid a hand on him.

Rage darkened Akihito Kuroda's face.

"*Never utter that man's name in this house!*" he hissed. "In fact, I would prefer it if you never spoke again." He glared at Ogawa, who looked equally stunned by the old man's action. "As of now, Haruki is grounded until further notice. I will hold you personally responsible if he somehow manages to leave this estate, is that understood?"

"Yes, boss," Ogawa muttered stiffly.

"Now, get out of my sight, both of you!"

Haruki walked out of the room in a daze, unheeding of the stares of the guards outside. There was no doubt they would have overheard what had just transpired.

"He hit me," he mumbled to Ogawa. "That's the first time he's ever done that."

"Why didn't you tell him what happened at the hotel?" The bodyguard blew out an exasperated sigh. "If you'd explained—"

A cynical chuckle left Haruki's lips. "Seriously? You think I should have told him that demons killed his first son and heir, and that his second son is some kind of monster too? Besides, he'd never believe me!"

Ogawa frowned. "You're not a monster."

"Oh yeah?" Haruki retorted. "Then how do you explain how I did what I did back there? Or why this—" he glanced at the bracelet on his right wrist, "this *thing* changed into a flaming sword?!"

"I can't," Ogawa said. "But that still doesn't mean you're a monster." He put a hand on Haruki's shoulder and stopped him in his tracks, his expression growing contrite. "Look, I know I've been hard on you all these years. We all have. But you risked your life to save your men. Not just today, but back in Chicago too, when we fought Serena Blake. And, unlike the demons we encountered today, I did not sense anything evil about that sword, or you for that matter." He faltered. "You are a worthy heir to the Kuroda Group. As worthy as Yashiro was."

Haruki remained silent as they headed toward his suite, too dumbfounded by Ogawa's words to speak.

"You need to talk to Artemus Steele," the bodyguard said. "I have a feeling he and his people will be able to tell you what happened to you back there. Besides, you saw his sword and the one Drake Hunter was holding. Their weapons were similar to yours."

Haruki ran a hand through his hair and sighed. "I know. But Artemus will have to wait."

Ogawa narrowed his eyes. "Why?"

"Because I need to go have a word with the head of the L.A. Triad."

~

"WHY DID YOU ORDER US TO WITHDRAW?" TIAN GAO asked with a scowl. "I could have dealt with those people on my own."

Delacourt bit back a sigh as he gazed at Ba'al's newest general. Tian Gao was slouched on his expensive leather couch and had already downed half a bottle of whiskey.

Maybe I should have killed him after all.

It was Delacourt who had contacted the head of their organization last month to inform him of the awakening of a powerful demon in L.A. And it was he who had found Tian Gao naked and bathed in blood behind the building where he'd killed and feasted on the bodies of half a dozen men after his transformation.

Delacourt knew from his own awakening many years past that only a demon commander was powerful enough to deal with a newly revived general. The demons who had come to attend to him when he himself had awakened had all died, victims of the insane bloodlust that had filled him at the time. It was a demon commander, the first of their kind in fact, who had finally managed to subdue him and return his mind to a state where he could actually comprehend what had happened to him.

Tian Gao's demon was one of the most powerful generals to awaken in recent years. More powerful even than Jade Q, Erik Park's righthand woman and lover.

Still, power does not necessarily equate to intelligence.

"I believe you would have found them hard to handle," he told the grouchy demon in a light tone. "They killed one of our commanders and hundreds of our brethren in New York a short while ago. And I most definitely would advise you never to go up against Messieurs Steele and Hunter on your own, Tian Gao."

"Who?" the Triad gang leader said.

Delacourt rubbed his forehead and felt his normally unshakeable disposition fray at the edges slightly. "The blond guy with the shiny sword and the man with the dark sword and shield. Drake Hunter, in particular, is someone who should not come to any harm at our hands."

Tian Gao raised an insolent eyebrow. "And why is that?"

"Because he's important to Ba'al," Delacourt replied. He took a sip of his whiskey and leaned back in his chair. "Now, tell me about Haruki Kuroda."

CHAPTER TWENTY-ONE

Artemus stared at the flaming torches atop the imposing walls of the immense, two-story, traditional Japanese mansion they were approaching.

"Whoa," Drake murmured. "The kid's rich."

"What did you expect?" Serena said. "He's practically Japanese mafia royalty."

The Kuroda estate sat on fifty acres of land in one of Malibu's most expensive zip codes and consisted of a main house and a variety of smaller secondary properties grouped around the principal mansion. It was through Serena and Nate's connections that they'd discovered the elusive location of the home of the head of the Kuroda Group.

Four guards in dark suits and bearing automatic firearms stood outside the wide otemon gate. They straightened when the two SUVs pulled to a stop in front of them, their hands tightening on their weapons and orange light from the paper lanterns above their heads dancing across their stiff faces.

Artemus frowned when he stepped out of the vehicle with the others.

Something's got them rattled.

He pasted an affable smile across his face. "Hi. We're here to see Haruki."

The guards glanced at one another.

"I'm afraid that's impossible," one of them said.

"I'm sure if you tell him our names, he'll—" Artemus started.

The man scowled and raised his firearm slightly.

"Master Haruki is not allowed any visitors right now," he said in a stony voice. "He has been grounded by Master Kuroda."

"Grounded?" Drake made a face. "What is he, five?"

The guards' expressions grew more aloof.

"Is Renji Ogawa here?" Serena said.

Surprise flashed on the men's faces.

"You know our boss?" one of them said.

"Yeah," Serena said. "I kicked his—I mean, we met him a few days ago."

The first guard who'd spoken frowned. "Mr. Ogawa is also indisposed right now. If you have no other business here, I kindly request that you leave."

"Artemus?" Callie said quietly as they headed back to the SUV.

He glanced at her. "Yeah?"

"I don't think Haruki's here."

Smokey's voice rose inside Artemus's head.

My sister is right. I do not detect the boy's energy.

Artemus frowned. It was becoming evident to him that Callie and Smokey could sense an energy signature that was similar to theirs much more easily than he could. He concentrated. His eyes widened with consternation when he failed to detect the otherwordly presence he'd discerned that morning at the hotel. He looked at Drake.

"I can't feel him either," his brother said.

～

"I KNOW I'VE SAID THIS BEFORE, BUT THIS IS A BAD idea," Ogawa grumbled. "I will definitely lose a finger over this."

Haruki knotted his bow tie before grabbing his dinner jacket from the trunk of the car they'd stolen after their escape from the Kuroda estate. "This is the only thing I can think to do right now. And I'll make sure you keep all ten fingers."

Haruki had been surprised when Ogawa had shown him the second escape tunnel that had been built under the property in case its occupants ever needed to make a swift retreat. Its location was known only to Akihito Kuroda and the head of security of the Kuroda Group.

He studied the property three hundred feet up the hill from where they'd parked. Bright lights dotted the extensive grounds and highlighted the sleek lines of the sprawling, contemporary, flat-roofed mansion that was home to one of Hollywood's most famous movie producers. Limos and town cars were pulling up in front of the gates, where a team of black-suited men stood guard and a hostess welcomed guests.

It was Ogawa who'd discovered where Qing Shan Liao, the head of the L.A. Triad, would be that evening. The man was listed as a guest at the party currently in full swing in the movie producer's residence. A patron of the arts, the Triad head was apparently an ardent fan of this particular man's films and had contributed financially to several of his blockbuster productions.

Haruki climbed inside the car with Ogawa.

"Are you ready?" he said in a hard voice.

"Not really," the bodyguard replied morosely, pressing the ignition.

The low roar of the Maserati's engine drew covetous eyes as it pulled up outside the metal security gates. Haruki stepped out with Ogawa, took the keys off the bodyguard, and cast them nonchalantly at a nearby valet.

"Here," he said with an arrogant smile. "Park this, will you?"

The guy gulped and nodded jerkily, his awestruck gaze taking in the streamlined shape of the luxury sports car.

Haruki kept the cocky smirk plastered across his face and strolled up to the hostess at a leisurely pace, his hands in the pockets of his tuxedo trousers.

"I'm not on the guest list, but I'm sure your boss will agree that I should not be turned away," he said to the pretty brunette looking at him with a quizzical expression.

The woman's eyes grew wary. She glanced at Ogawa.

"Are you paparazzi?" she said sharply.

One of the guards stared hard at Haruki before whispering something to the man beside him. The other guy's eyes widened. He dipped his chin, some of the color draining from his face.

The first guard came forward and spoke rapidly in the hostess's ear. The woman blinked.

"I'm—I'm so sorry for not recognizing you, Mr. Kuroda!" she stammered. "I'm afraid I'm new to the city. If I had known—"

"Don't worry," Haruki said with a relaxed wave of his hand. He winked at the woman. "I won't tell if you won't."

A blush stained the woman's cheeks.

Haruki could practically feel Ogawa trying not to roll his eyes behind him. The hostess ushered them into the grounds of the property.

"Okay, now that we're in, what exactly do you plan to do to Liao?" the bodyguard murmured as they headed up the paved driveway to a rectangular courtyard dominated by a modern water fountain.

"Talk," Haruki said in a determined voice. "I only want to talk to him."

They entered the residence and were immediately engulfed in a cloud of cigar smoke and expensive perfume. Haruki surveyed the crowd of A-list stars and movie moguls standing and lounging in an immense hallway and a sunken lounge that spanned half the width of the house before opening onto a terrace with a pool and gardens decked out with fairy lights.

"Christ, I think half of Hollywood is here," Ogawa mumbled, staring at an actor who was currently featured in the number one movie at the box office.

"Keep your eyes out for Liao."

Haruki took a glass of champagne off a passing waiter and headed farther inside the house.

They drew curious gazes as they walked around, the other guests evidently trying to pinpoint where they knew him from. Many studied Haruki with lingering looks, their eyes telling him they liked what they were seeing.

Haruki remained unfazed. He had bigger fish to fry tonight. Besides, he wasn't someone who was easily star-struck.

They finally tracked Liao down to a gazebo in the gardens. The head of the Triad was in deep conversation with a man Haruki dimly recognized as having seen on the red carpet on TV.

"That's the movie producer," Ogawa murmured in Haruki's ear as they approached the private area.

The two men paused mid-flow when Haruki climbed the steps of the arbor.

"Grant," Haruki said, flashing a smile at the movie producer and shaking the bewildered man's hand. "Great party. I'm sorry to interrupt your talk, but would it be possible for me to take a few minutes of Mr. Liao's time? I promise I'll have him back to you soon."

Liao studied Haruki with an inscrutable expression while the movie producer glanced between the two of them, still mystified.

"It's okay, Grant," the head of the Triad said quietly. "We can continue where we left off in a moment."

"Sure. Give me a shout when you're done."

The guy rose and headed across the gardens toward his other guests.

Haruki took the seat he'd vacated, conscious of the guarded stares and stiff stances of the four Triad bodyguards hovering close to Liao.

"You have guts, kid," Liao said, his voice hardening. He took a puff on his cigar and sat back in his chair, smoke curling out of his nostrils and the corners of his mouth as he exhaled. "Does your father know you're here?"

"No, he doesn't," Haruki replied quietly. "And I would rather he not find out either." He glanced at Liao's bodyguards. "What I'm about to discuss is highly sensitive. May I ask that all your men bar the one you trust the most step out for this?"

Surprise flashed in the older man's eyes. The guy next

to the Triad head frowned and whispered urgently in his ear.

"It's fine, Sho," Liao murmured. "You stay." He glanced at his other guards. "Leave us."

The men bowed their heads respectfully and left the gazebo.

"Well, what is it that's so 'sensitive' that you could not talk freely in front of my men, Kuroda?" Liao asked coldly.

Haruki watched him for a moment.

"I know who killed my brother," he said. "I think you know the identity of that man too." His knuckles whitened where he'd fisted his hands on his knees, his throat working as he struggled to utter the words he needed to say next. "I also believe you had nothing to do with it."

CHAPTER TWENTY-TWO

OGAWA STARTLED BEHIND HARUKI AS THE RELUCTANT admission echoed around the gazebo.

"What are you saying?" the bodyguard said in a shocked voice. "You know full well the Triad—"

"Think about it," Haruki said. "No other members of our organization have suffered any ill at the hands of the Triad since the day Yashiro and Riuji were murdered. And Mr. Liao—" he observed the silent man across from him with a faint frown, "has done his utmost to keep the peace between the Triad and the Kuroda Group. If he really wanted a war with us, the streets of L.A. would be red with the blood of our men by now."

Ogawa clenched his jaw, his expression still mutinous.

"Your young master is correct," Liao said. "I did not order the murder of Yashiro Kuroda or your men."

Haruki stared at him, surprised by the unexpected confession.

Liao sighed.

"Things are never as straightforward as they seem," the man said in a tired voice. "You see, Tian Gao is the son of my youngest sister. Not only that, he is a highly valued member of our L.A. organization and a good friend of the brother of the current Dragon Head of the Hong Kong Triad, who happens to be my direct superior. In time, Tian Gao aims to take my seat as the head of the West Coast Triad." He stared pointedly at Haruki. "You understand that although I am aware of his unforgivable actions, I cannot make an example of him without incurring the wrath of those nearest and dearest to me, don't you?"

The Triad head's words resonated inside Haruki's mind. Realization slowly dawned as he gazed at the older man.

"But—*I* can?" he said, stunned.

The Triad bodyguard's eyes widened as he stared at his leader.

An awkward silence filled the gazebo.

"Is that what you're saying?" Haruki asked stiffly. "Are you granting me—" he paused and glanced at Ogawa, "granting *us* your official permission to kill Tian Gao? And there shall be no reprisals against the Kuroda Group if we do?"

Liao grimaced. "Official is taking things a bit far. But a revenge killing is something our Dragon Head would understand." He shrugged. "An eye for an eye. A life for a life. That is the way of our world." He paused. "Besides, as strange as this may sound, I actually had a soft spot for your brother. Yashiro was a gentleman through and through. He would have made a great head of the Kuroda Group."

Haruki looked at Ogawa and saw the same shock reflected in his eyes.

A muscle jumped in his jawline as he turned to face Liao once more. "I'm afraid I already tried this morning."

"Tried what?" Liao said.

Haruki sighed and rubbed his forehead. "To kill Tian Gao."

Liao frowned. "You mean, you failed?"

"Yes," Haruki murmured, the crushing defeat he'd suffered that morning bringing forth a surge of shame and anger once more. "There's more going on with Tian Gao than you know."

He leaned forward and started talking in a low voice. Liao's eyes widened as Haruki recounted a tale of demons and devils. Of the evil that walked the Earth in the guise of ordinary men and women. Of Ba'al and Tian Gao's apparent affiliation to them.

"You seriously expect me to believe that?" the head of the L.A. Triad asked, aghast, when Haruki finished speaking. "That—that utter *fabrication?*" Anger darkened his face. "Who do you take me for, boy?!"

Haruki clenched his teeth, frustration gnawing at him. "Look, I know what it sounds like. Believe me, the first time I heard this story, I scoffed at it too." He swallowed. "It all sounds far-fetched, but trust me, it's the truth. And we're going to need your help to defeat them."

Liao scowled. "My help?"

"Show him," Ogawa said brusquely.

Haruki gave the bodyguard a puzzled look.

"The bracelet." Ogawa indicated the juzu beads on Haruki's right wrist. "Show him."

Haruki blinked. "I—"

Liao glanced between the two of them. "Show me what?"

Haruki studied the Triad head's suspicious eyes.

Ogawa is right. This is the fastest way to convince him.

Haruki rose slowly to his feet, looked around the

gardens to make sure no curious eyes were directed their way, took a shallow breath, and concentrated.

This time, he registered where the heat that filled his body was coming from. It had happened too fast in Chicago and back at the hotel today for him to notice, but he was certain now that it arose from his back. More precisely, it seemed to be centered around the mark that wrapped around his spine. A mark he'd come by when he was still in Japan.

The juzu beads trembled around his wrist as an unholy energy poured through him. The dragon's eyes glowed red.

The bracelet transformed into a pale, flaming sword with a gilded hilt, the blade slicing the air with a faint hum.

Liao startled and jumped out of his seat. His bodyguard cursed and drew his gun.

Haruki ignored them and stared at the weapon in his hand. It was his first time getting a close look at it. He hesitated before touching the sword reverently with his fingertips, awed by the power thrumming through it.

The flames did not burn his skin.

It's beautiful.

"What is that?" Liao asked harshly. His face hardened. "Is this some kind of illusion?" He looked warily around the garden. "Are you trying to fool me?"

"No," Haruki said. "This is a divine weapon."

He blinked, shocked by the words he had just unconsciously uttered.

How did I know that?

That was when Haruki felt it once more. The heartbeat that did not belong to him. It thumped through his chest, an alien drumming that rose in magnitude until it overtook his own heartbeat. Something slithered behind his eyes. He gasped as the world turned into a kaleidoscope of bright hues and everything around him became as crisp and as clear as if it were the brightest, sunniest day.

Liao took a step back, the color draining from his face.

"Your eyes," he mumbled.

Haruki brought a hand to his face and turned to Ogawa.

The bodyguard drew a sharp breath. "Master Haruki."

Panic gripped Haruki. "What's wrong with my eyes?"

They are coming.

Haruki nearly jumped out of his skin at the deep, gravelly voice that had just resonated inside his skull. He knew instinctively it belonged to the fearsome creature he could sense behind his eyes. The hairs rose on his arms. An ominous feeling washed over him. His stomach dropped as coils of darkness pooled in the air around them.

Ogawa swore.

Haruki followed his gaze to the three Triad bodyguards who had stepped out of the gazebo. The same coal-black strands were forming above the men's heads, crowning them with a foul aura. Shudders racked their bodies, as if they were in the grip of a seizure. Their eyes rolled back in their heads before turning obsidian from edge to edge, their pupils morphing into eerie circles of yellow light. Their bodies transformed the next instant.

"What the—?"

The color drained from Liao's face as he stared at the monstrous forms his men had taken.

The demons charged.

"Get back!" Haruki shouted.

He rushed in front of Liao and his remaining bodyguard, slashed the first demon across the chest, and decapitated the other two. Startled shouts rang out across the gardens, the sudden commotion drawing the eyes of the other guests. They headed toward the gazebo, their faces curious.

"Great!" Ogawa snarled, his gun in hand. "Those idiots probably think this is some kind of stunt!"

Shadows thickened around the gazebo. More demons appeared out of the night, their insubstantial shapes trembling before materializing fully out of thin air.

Ogawa blanched. "Shit!"

"Are these the creatures you told me about?" Liao said hoarsely.

Haruki gripped the sword in both hands and glanced at the shocked Triad head. "Yes."

Liao looked from the ghastly apparitions to Haruki and the blade he held. "If they are demons, then what does that make you?"

Haruki studied the horde of fiendish creatures around them with a scowl.

"Someone who detests them," he said grimly.

He knew even as he spoke the words that they represented the quintessence of what he was and why he had been granted the right to use the weapon in his hands.

Haruki blinked.

Now, why did I just think that?

The creature inside him spoke once more.

It is because you are beginning to see the truth.

For a moment, Haruki glimpsed the shape of the beast within. A shiver raced down his spine at the fearsome specter coiled around his very soul. He swallowed.

Lend me your strength!

The beast's eyes glowed with a feral light.

As you wish.

"Delacourt was right about you," someone said in a low

growl behind him.

Haruki's heart contracted painfully. He spun around and stared at the demon who'd just appeared between him and Ogawa.

"Tian Gao?" Liao whispered, his face ashen as he stared at his nephew.

Tian Gao turned and smirked at the Triad head. "Hello, Uncle."

He knocked the older man aside with a violent swing of his clawed hand. Liao sailed through the air and smashed into one of the gazebo supports with a harsh grunt.

"Master Liao!" the Triad bodyguard shouted, rushing to his leader's side.

One of the guests screamed. Panicked shouts followed as the crowd finally realized something was very wrong and started to disperse.

"Ogawa, protect Liao!" Haruki barked.

Tian Gao narrowed his eyes at Haruki as the bodyguard headed over to Liao.

"We are not here to fight you," the demon said. "We want you to come with us."

Haruki's skin quivered as power poured through him. His back and head started to itch. Heat pooled inside his stomach.

"And why the hell would I do that?" he snarled.

He startled when wisps of smoke curled around his face from his mouth and nose. Flashes of light on the sword drew his gaze. Symbols appeared on the flat of the blade, signs that he felt he should recognize but didn't.

A smug smile twisted Tian Gao's face. "Because you're a Guardian. And that—" he pointed at the sword, "is your key."

CHAPTER TWENTY-THREE

"East is a *very* general direction, Callie!" Artemus said as they raced through the city.

"Look, I'm trying my best here!" she retorted with a scowl.

Nate veered sharply around a van, clenched his jaw when he saw the fourteen-wheeler coming at him, and swerved back into the right lane. Isabelle stayed close on his tail in the second SUV.

They'd just passed Santa Monica and were headed into Beverly Hills.

Artemus steadied himself against the back door and the roof of the SUV as Nate changed gears and zigzagged through the traffic at breakneck speed.

He glanced at Smokey. "What about you, Fuzzface?"

Smokey's eyes glowed with a red light.

He is somewhere up high.

Drake stared at the dark elevations on the left of the highway. "He's in the mountains?"

Callie drew a sharp breath. Smokey shivered.

"What is it?" Serena asked, gazing at them in the rearview mirror.

"His power just surged," Callie said grimly. "There!" She pointed at a sign coming up on the highway. "Take that exit!"

Nate cut across three lanes and barreled onto the ramp amidst a cacophony of horns. Hollywood Hills loomed in front of them half a mile later. They accelerated up the incline.

The faint sounds of sirens reached Artemus's ears. He looked over his shoulder and saw the light bars of half a dozen patrol cars racing across the valley toward the mountains. More appeared in the distance.

"Somehow, I don't think they're for us," Drake said.

"Turn right!" Callie barked.

Nate spun the steering wheel and sent them careening into a stomach-lurching, one-eighty spin. He dropped gears and headed briskly up a winding road dotted with private, gated estates. Artemus frowned when he sensed a heavy concentration of demonic energy somewhere ahead. They rounded a corner in a screech of tires and turned into a street lined with cars.

"Well, I think we found the place," Serena said grimly.

Three hundred feet up the hill, dozens of elegantly-dressed people were running out of a large, modern residence, their panicked screams echoing in the night.

Haruki ducked beneath a spate of clawed hands and swung his sword. Two demons screeched as the blade sliced their arms off at the wrist. They fell back toward the horde of creatures amassed around the gazebo, their obsidian eyes flaring with pain and hate.

Tian Gao stood behind them and watched the battle with an amused expression. Haruki glared at him, his breaths coming in steady pants. He'd already slayed half a dozen demons and injured as many in the last few minutes.

This bastard is toying with me!

He gritted his teeth and glanced at Liao, Ogawa, and the Triad bodyguard where they stood behind him. Fury and frustration had replaced the fear in Liao's eyes. They'd tried firing their guns at the demons but to no avail; their bullets were useless against the creatures.

At least Tian Gao's left them alone for now.

The words the demon had spoken a short while back resonated through Haruki's mind once more. He did not know what this guardian or key thing was about but he sensed the beast inside him did. His eyesight was still behaving strangely. Though not as bright as before, he could see everything around him as if it were a slightly cloudy day. The itching on his back and scalp was also steadily getting worse. And other parts of him had started to prickle too.

Three demons darted out of the throng and bounded toward him.

Haruki stabbed one of them in the heart, kicked the second one in the stomach, and twisted on his heels to decapitate the third. The creature evaded his strike and came at him with a piercing scream.

Haruki raised his arm to block the blow headed for his neck. Sparks erupted when the demon's claws made contact with his hand.

Both Haruki and the creature stared at the silver scales that had appeared on his skin like a shield. Haruki recovered first and thrust his sword through the demon's heart. The creature slumped to the ground and assumed the shape of its dead human host.

Tian Gao's smile faded.

Haruki braced himself as the foul energy around him intensified.

Shit. If they all come at me at once—

"Enough play time," Tian Gao growled. "Get him."

"Master Haruki!" Ogawa shouted.

"*Stay back!*" Haruki yelled.

His knuckles whitened on the gilded hilt of his sword. His fists glinted as more scales grew across his skin. They bloomed up his arms under the tuxedo until they covered his nape, shoulders, and back. The heat inside his belly expanded and raced up his chest to his throat.

"Hey, need a hand over there, kid?" someone called out from the direction of the house.

Artemus slowed as he headed into the gardens. Haruki stood at the head of a gazebo, in front of three men he was evidently protecting. They were surrounded by a pack of demons.

Tian Gao towered to the right of the crowd. He turned and glared at Artemus. The demon's gaze shifted to the figures beside him. Surprise widened his obsidian eyes.

"Is that really Haruki?" Callie said, a guttural growl underscoring her voice.

She was in full Chimera form, her scepter clutched in her right hand. Smokey padded next to her, his hellhound shape merging with the night but for his glowing red eyes.

"Yes," Artemus murmured, his gaze focused on the creature with the flaming sword.

"What is he?" Elton said, his tone fascinated even as his grip tightened on his modified Beretta.

"I don't know."

A name floated at the back of Artemus's mind. It danced away before he could decipher it. Drake stopped beside him, his red gaze similarly centered on Haruki.

The Kuroda heir's pupils were vertical slits aglow with an orange light. His face looked tight, as if the flesh had been stretched over the bones, rendering him an almost serpent-like appearance. Tendrils of smoke curled from his nostrils and lips. Something was shining faintly over his chest and abdomen, under the tuxedo he wore. And the skin on his hands had sprouted silver scales that Artemus was willing to bet would be unbreakable.

Serena and Nate depressed the buttons on the black discs they'd placed on their chests. The devices flattened and expanded into nanorobot, liquid-armor combat suits that covered them from the neck down in a handful of seconds. They unsheathed their knives, their faces deadly, focused masks.

Artemus smiled grimly. "Let's go kill some demons."

CHAPTER TWENTY-FOUR

HARUKI STARED AT THE GROUP HEADED FOR THE HORDE of demons.

Artemus had drawn his pale sword once more while Drake held his darker blade in hand, his shield covering his left arm.

But it was the creatures next to them that captured Haruki's attention in a heartbeat.

Padding beside Artemus was a giant dog some four feet tall and as black as night. His pupils were circles radiating an unholy, crimson light and his open jaws exposed the most wicked fangs Haruki had ever seen. On the other side of Drake was a woman who looked vaguely like Callie Stone. Except no human female had glowing jade eyes, clawed hands and feet, hair made of hundreds of hissing golden snakes, flamed-tipped horns on their forehead, and a giant serpent protruding from their tail bone.

The beast inside Haruki roused when he sensed their presence.

Our brethren are here.

The creatures around the gazebo turned to face the

newcomers, their animal growls filling the air. The night grew blacker still as more malevolent shapes materialized out of the gloom and descended upon the gardens.

ARTEMUS THRUST HIS BLADE AT THE DEMON DROPPING on him from the sky to his left. The creature impaled himself violently on the shimmering sword before slumping to the ground, dragging the weapon with him as he transformed into a man once more. Artemus drew his sword out of the corpse and leaned back to avoid the talons headed for his heart.

Smokey barreled into a group of demons, knocked them to the ground, and pinned them down while he tore at their throats. Black blood splashed across his muzzle and his hide while his acid drool melted their skin and flesh.

The horde snarled and screeched as Elton and his team peppered them with silver-leaded bullets. Artemus raised the weapon Karl LeBlanc had made for him, a stainless-steel gun blessed with a prayer that could send demons back to Hell itself.

The creatures he fired at froze in their tracks, their pupils widening as their bodies became brief, glowing shapes that exploded into clouds of ash.

SERENA JUMPED IN THE AIR, KNEED A DEMON IN THE throat, and slashed the necks of the ones leaping at her from her left and right as she fell to the ground. She landed lightly on her feet, evaded the claws aimed at her eyes, and flipped backward onto her hands, her boots smashing into the jaws of her attackers. She touched down next to the swimming pool and was headed into the fray when two demons slammed into her and carried her into the water.

They hit the surface hard and plunged toward the bottom.

Serena's blades slipped out of her grasp as she wrestled with the creatures coiled around her, their talons scraping her combat suit where they tried to gouge her flesh. The liquid-armor suit absorbed their attacks. She reached for her guns and gritted her teeth when the weapons were knocked out of her hands. Blood misted the water as a claw found the back of her exposed wrist. The nanorobots in her body healed the wound in the blink of an eye.

Her feet touched the pool bed. Serena braced herself and heaved the demons off her. The creatures started to rise through the water, their uncanny eyes flaring at her superhuman strength. One of them twisted down, wrapped his legs around her throat, and grabbed her temples with his clawed hands.

The tendons in Serena's neck screamed as he tugged on her head. A bubble of air escaped her lips. She sagged to her knees and blocked the talons of the demon trying to tear her gut open. Stars exploded in front of her eyes when she yanked him close and headbutted him in the face.

The demon's mouth opened on a grunt, black blood flowing out of his broken, misshapen nose. His eyes widened when he accidentally inhaled water. He kicked off toward the surface, gasping in panic.

Serena grabbed the thighs of the demon strangling her at the same time that he was endeavoring to rip her head off her body and tried to pry his limbs open. He tightened his vicious grip. She cursed internally as her lungs started to ache from the lack of oxygen.

Light glinted on something at the bottom of the pool.

Serena clenched her jaw and managed to lower her gaze a fraction, her heartbeat pounding dully in her ears. She saw the dagger by her left knee, kicked it up, and grabbed the blade as it floated past her.

The demon on her shoulders screamed as she stabbed him in the left thigh. Black liquid tainted the waters around her. She twisted the blade.

DRAKE DEFLECTED SEVERAL BLOWS WITH HIS SHIELD AND lobbed the heads off three demons as he headed toward where he'd seen Serena disappear. His heart twisted with fear when he saw the creature climbing out of the water. He saw the dark shapes at the bottom of pool, scowled, and thrust his sword through the heart of the demon rising to his feet with a bleeding, broken nose.

Drake was about to dive into the pool when the water turned murky with demon blood. Serena broke through the surface with a gasp a few seconds later. Relief flooded him. He grabbed her arm and hauled her out.

"Thanks!" the super soldier panted. She bent over, spat out a mouthful of water, and wiped her lips with a grimace. "Yuck. Demon blood tastes disgusting!" She straightened and frowned at the eerie shapes pooling out of the darkness around them. "These assholes just keep coming, don't they?"

"That's because they have a vested interest in being here," Drake said, his gaze finding Haruki. His eyes widened. "Shit! That guy's gonna—"

CHAPTER TWENTY-FIVE

HARUKI'S BREATHS CAME IN HARSH PANTS AS HE FENDED off the rabid creatures swooping onto the gazebo. Ogawa and Liao's bodyguard slashed at a couple of demons with their knives where they stood protecting the Triad head. Both men were sweating hard and bleeding from the cuts they had sustained.

Damn it! Even with Artemus and the others here, there are just too many of them!

The mass of fiends in front of him heaved as someone broke through their ranks. Nate appeared. The giant man punched a demon in the jaw so hard he practically left an imprint of his fist in the creature's flesh. The demon's head snapped back with an audible crack. Nate kneed another in the stomach, kicked a third in the face, and slashed the throats of two more, his movements swift and sure. Talons raked his left cheek. He grabbed the head of the demon who'd wounded him and broke the creature's neck with a twist of his hands.

Haruki stared. Nate's wounds were knitting together

smoothly, just as Serena's had when Haruki had cut her with his knife the night they first met in Chicago.

"What the hell are you people?"

He looked across the gardens to where Drake was pulling Serena out of the pool. Nate front kicked a demon in the groin and followed Haruki's gaze to the brunette.

"We're your friends," he said. "For now."

"Master Haruki!" Ogawa shouted. "*Watch out!*"

A shadow fell over Haruki. He turned and gasped as a large, clawed hand wrapped around his throat and lifted him bodily into the air.

A scowl darkened Tian Gao's features as he held Haruki up at face level.

Ogawa rushed toward the demon.

"No!" Nate grabbed the bodyguard's arm and pulled him to a stop. "You can't take him on."

Tian Gao smirked at the two men. "That's right." His obsidian eyes locked on Haruki once more. "You're coming with me."

Haruki gritted his teeth. "Like hell I am!"

He gripped his sword with both hands and stabbed Tian Gao in the gut.

The demon roared. "*That hurt, you little runt!*"

He yanked the blade out of his body and struck Haruki hard across the face. Black dots swarmed Haruki's vision as his neck twisted painfully to the side. He shook his head weakly and looked around in time to see the shadows thicken next to them.

Pure darkness was pooling out of the night. It formed eerie, black shapes that melded and merged until they became a thick, black line as tall as the demon.

The strange phenomenon tore open with a loud, ripping sound that reverberated through Haruki's very bones. Crimson light appeared in the crack that split through its center. The fissure widened, its sickening glow throbbing with intense, demonic energy. Haruki's heart clenched with fear.

Tian Gao turned and headed into the light.

Something flashed across the gardens and pierced the demon's left shoulder. He grunted and released Haruki.

CALLIE RAISED HER HAND AND CAUGHT THE SCEPTER AS it curved through the air and returned to her grasp, the rod slick with the blood of the creatures she had slayed. Tian Gao turned. The beast inside her growled when his obsidian eyes landed on her.

She opened her jaws and released a sonic roar. Nate, Haruki, and the men behind them winced and covered their ears. Tian Gao blinked, his body growing still. Callie's breath caught when he broke the hold of the paralyzing blast and took a step forward.

He is strong.

She clenched her teeth at the Chimera's words.

Tian Gao descended the steps of the gazebo and headed toward her, his expression murderous. Callie braced herself as his giant shadow engulfed her smaller frame. She blocked his first blow with the scepter, sucked in air, and let out a jet of fierce, bright flames from her mouth.

Fire engulfed Tian Gao. He stumbled back toward some bushes. Callie panted slightly as she watched the blaze abate. Surprise jolted her when the flames dissipated to reveal the demon still standing.

Tian Gao straightened from his defensive crouch and

examined his scorched skin curiously. A savage smile twisted his face.

"Is that all you have, beast?" he spat.

The ground trembled under Callie's feet as the demon charged. She narrowed her eyes and spun the scepter in front of her, her marks quivering and her power surging as the beast within her rose.

A black shape leapt through the air from her right, struck Tian Gao in the flank, and brought the demon to the ground.

A wild growl rumbled from Smokey's chest as he closed his jaws on the demon's injured shoulder. Tian Gao grabbed the hellhound around the chest and tore the beast off him. Smokey jumped back, dropped the gory chunk of flesh he'd ripped out with his jowls, and pawed the ground, his body swelling by another foot and his eyes turning a molten gold as he drew on his power.

"*Why, you—*"

Tian Gao jumped to his feet and rushed the hellhound.

Drake bolted in front of Smokey.

His eyes were glowing, scarlet circles filled with an untamed force. His sword had grown and darkened, the blade's edges twisting into vicious, jagged teeth. The shield on his left arm had similarly dulled, the metal now a dark gray.

Artemus appeared behind Tian Gao, his blade glimmering with a growing white haze even as it lengthened and widened. Golden light flashed in his eyes for a moment.

"You sure you can take all of us on?" he asked the demon in a deadly voice.

Callie's heart thumped as she felt the bonds that linked all of them thicken and grow as they faced down the giant demon. Even Haruki's unknown beast joined in, his life force an orange thread pulsing with savage energy as it entwined around theirs. For a moment, she thought she glimpsed the creature's dim shape.

Tian Gao scowled, his clawed hands fisting at his sides. The demon's corrupt energy escalated as he prepared to do battle.

The night split open with a loud rending noise. Daniel Delacourt stepped out of a rift next to Tian Gao and took hold of his arm.

"Let's go," he said sternly.

Tian Gao growled and started to struggle in the man's grasp. "I can still defeat—"

Callie stiffened as the air around them grew heavy. Drake and Artemus tensed. Smokey's eyes flashed red.

A loathsome miasma materialized around Delacourt.

The hairs rose on Callie's arms as the blond man's face darkened and warped, the demon inside him emerging for a fleeting moment.

"*You will do as you are told!*" he bellowed at Tian Gao.

The lights dotting the gardens exploded. Windows shattered in the house. The demons around them cowered to the ground.

"Now, retreat!" Delacourt ordered.

The creatures faded into the shadows, their eyes glinting with fear. Even Tian Gao looked subdued as he headed into the rift ahead of Delacourt.

The blond man stopped and studied the group scattered around the gardens. "You may have won this battle. But we *will* win the war."

His cold gaze landed on Haruki before he turned and vanished inside the rift. Sirens echoed across the hill in the stark silence that befell them.

CHAPTER TWENTY-SIX

"CERBERUS?" HARUKI REPEATED. HE STARED AT THE rabbit perched on Callie's lap. "As in, the Hound of Hades?"

Callie nodded. "Ah-huh."

Haruki arched an eyebrow at the blonde. "And you're the Chimera?"

"Yup," Callie said.

"For someone who had glowing eyes and grew scales a short while back, you sure as hell look skeptical, kid," Serena muttered.

Haruki frowned. "It's a lot to digest. Not to mention it's not exactly normal. And, again, I'm not that much younger than you."

They were in a mansion that belonged to friends of Callie's, in Holmby Hills. After narrowly averting discovery by the police at the movie producer's house, Haruki had dispatched Ogawa to escort a shocked Liao home, while he accompanied Artemus and the others. The Triad head's last words to Haruki echoed in his mind.

"I don't know what happened here tonight. The

things—" the Triad head had paused, his expression troubled as he gazed from Haruki to Artemus and his group, "the things I witnessed will take some time to sink in." Liao's face had hardened briefly. "One thing I'm certain of. Tian Gao means to kill me. Whether it was going to be tonight or in the future, I don't know. It's clear his alliance is no longer with the Triad, but with these...these creatures!"

Elton's voice brought him back to the present. "Do you know the name of your sword?"

Haruki blinked, surprised. He glanced at the juzu bracelet on his wrist. The sword had resumed its original form shortly after the battle had ended.

"No. Should I?"

"I wonder if Otis would know," Artemis murmured.

"Who's Otis?" Haruki said.

"My assistant." Artemus glanced at Callie. "He knew the identity of our weapons."

"What about your beast?" Callie asked Haruki, her green eyes keen with interest.

The memory of the fearsome creature who'd spoken to him in the midst of his fight with the demons tonight washed over Haruki once more. With it came a stream of conflicting emotions. Gratitude. Curiosity. Apprehension. And an unexpected feeling of...belonging. A feeling that seemed as strange as the bonds of fellowship he could sense between himself and the people who'd entered his life in the last week.

The connection he felt with Callie, Artemus, Drake, and Smokey was stronger now than what he'd experienced back in Chicago, when they'd first met. Haruki couldn't shake the feeling that they were companions of sorts, bound together by a common fate and headed on a mysterious journey, the objectives and destination of which were yet to be determined.

"The beast?" he repeated.

"The one who lives inside you," Callie said doggedly. "The one whose powers are awakening."

Haruki hesitated. "What about him?"

"Ah," Artemus murmured. "So, it's a he."

"Do you know his name and what he is?" Drake asked.

Haruki frowned. "No." He looked at Callie. "What did you mean when you said awakening?"

"Remember when we told you we'd fought Ba'al before, in Chicago and in New York?" Artemus said.

"Yeah?"

"That was when Callie's powers as the Chimera started to manifest," Drake explained. "But it wasn't until she came in close contact with her gate that she and the weapon she wielded fully awakened."

"Gate?" Haruki said, confused. "What gate?"

Artemus spoke then. Back in Chicago, he had told Haruki of the cane that Callie's dead husband had purchased in Jerusalem two decades past. Of how her bringing the item to Elton LeBlanc's auction house a few weeks ago had triggered a chain of events that had brought all of them together and resulted in the discovery of the identity of the demonic organization that had started to make its presence felt around the world some twenty odd years ago.

He now told Haruki of the Vatican group that Elton and his team belonged to and how the Catholic Church had allied itself with hundreds of government and private organizations as well as other religious bodies around the world in their common cause to fight the demons. Finally, he related the circumstances that had led to Callie and

Nate's kidnapping and torture by Ba'al, and how Callie had been forced by one of Ba'al's commanders to attempt to open an arch that turned out to be a gate to Hell.

By the time Artemus finished talking, Haruki's heart was racing in his chest.

"A gate to Hell?" he said hoarsely.

"Yes," Drake said in a troubled tone.

Artemus glanced at the other man. Smokey's ears twitched as he too looked at Drake.

Haruki could not help but feel that a silent message had just passed between the three of them.

He studied Serena and Nate. "What about you? You're not normal."

"I'll forgive that rude comment for now," Serena said coolly. Her gaze moved briefly to the silent man beside her. "Nate and I are super soldiers."

Haruki startled. "Super soldiers? As in—what, some kind of enhanced human?"

"Yes," Serena replied. "We were designed in a lab some three decades ago. The...people who bioengineered us weren't just interested in producing super humans though. They combined human DNA with nanorobots to create an army of perfect killing machines." She paused. "They also used Immortal DNA."

Haruki stared, not sure if he'd heard her right. "Did you just say immortal?!"

"The less we talk about that stuff, the better," Isabelle muttered, frowning at Serena.

Haruki looked down at his hands, his mind abuzz from everything he'd just learned.

He swallowed before gazing at Callie once more. "You said you are the—the Guardian of the gate you found in

New York." He indicated the cane at her side. "And *that* is your key?"

"Yes," Callie said. "Although it's really the cane's true form that's the key."

"Its...true form?" Haruki said falteringly.

Callie nodded. "The Scepter of Gabriel."

A ringing started in Haruki's ears. "As in the—the *Archangel* from the Bible?"

"The very one," Serena muttered.

Artemus's expression grew concerned as he observed Haruki. "Hey, are you okay?"

Haruki nodded numbly, too stunned to speak for a moment. "Tian Gao—" He stopped, his heart thumping violently against his ribs. "Tian Gao said I am a Guardian and that the sword—" he stared at the bracelet Yashiro had given him, "the sword is my key. When Liao asked me what it was, I told him the sword was a divine weapon. I didn't even know I was going to say that until I did."

Taut silence descended around them.

"So, the Vatican was right," Elton murmured grimly. "There really *is* another gate in L.A."

Haruki stared blindly at the older man. "What happened to the one you found in New York?"

"It's with the Vatican," Elton replied. "Their experts are examining it as we speak. We hope it will give us clues to identifying the whereabouts of Ba'al's leader and their objectives."

"Isn't that kinda risky?" Haruki mumbled. "What if Ba'al finds the gate and tries to open it again?"

"They can't do that without me and the scepter," Callie said confidently.

"Besides, the Vatican has some...unusual allies who are

helping guard the gate," Elton said with a slightly troubled expression.

"I've been meaning to ask you something." Serena frowned at Haruki. "Do you have any marks?"

A jolt of surprise shot through him. "What do you mean?"

Serena indicated Callie, Artemus, and Drake. "They all have these marks on their bodies. They're not birthmarks but rather designs that appeared on all of them, the same night, in August 2017."

Haruki felt the blood drain from his face.

"August 2017?" he whispered.

Artemus leaned forward in his seat, his eyes taking on a zealous glint. "So, you have them too?"

Haruki hesitated before dipping his chin. He rose to his feet, stripped out of his tuxedo jacket and shirt, and turned.

"Whoa," Isabelle murmured. "That's a lot of tattoos."

Haruki's back was covered in the large, colorful motifs favored by the Yakuza. Wrapped around his spine, the only midnight-black design on his skin, was the mark he'd inherited one day during the third summer of his life, when he was still living with his ailing mother and his grandparents in Japan.

His family had panicked when they had first seen it. He'd awoken from a nap and told them his back felt itchy. Fearing he needed some kind of exorcism, they'd taken him to their Shinto shrine, only to have one of the priests tell them not to fear the mark. That it was a sign of something powerful and protective.

Light footsteps rose behind Haruki. He shivered as warm fingers danced down his spine and traced the dark lines.

"It's beautiful," Callie said quietly.

Haruki twisted on his heels to face her, his pulse hammering in his veins. She pulled her hair to the side and showed him the horned lion on her nape, before tucking the waistband of her jeans down slightly to reveal the snake at the bottom of her spine.

"Artemus and Drake have wings on their backs," she said with a gentle smile.

Haruki observed the two men before looking at Smokey. "Does he have marks too?"

Artemus sighed. "No. He just likes the form of my pet rabbit. The one he ate when I was six."

Smokey rubbed his nose with his paws, expression abashed.

"The symbols that appeared on your sword tonight," Callie said. "Do you know what they meant?"

Haruki shook his head. He'd almost forgotten about them.

"So, it's just as I suspected. Chances are your beast won't know their true meaning until you're close to your gate." Callie paused. "It's only when those sigils are translated that the key will be activated and the gate can be opened. It's also likely the time that you will fully awaken."

CHAPTER TWENTY-SEVEN

"It's gone?" Artemus stared at Ogawa. "What do you mean?"

"I mean it's gone," the bodyguard repeated. "As in, the shop is literally not there. A cousin of one of our men lives in Hong Kong. He went to look for it today, at my request. He said it's just a vacant parking lot. That the place where Master Yashiro bought the bracelet never existed."

It was past midnight and they were on their way downtown once more. Haruki's bodyguard had arrived at the mansion in Holmby Hills in the last hour, having safely escorted Liao home.

"By the way," Ogawa told Haruki as the SUV moved briskly along the Interstate, "needless to say, your father is furious. Liao said he was going to call him." The bodyguard's expression turned morose. "I'm definitely gonna lose that finger."

Haruki remained silent, his expression troubled.

Artemus frowned and gazed out the window.

The more he thought about it, the more there were too many coincidences for his liking. How Ronald Stone had ended up purchasing a mysterious artifact destined for a woman he wouldn't meet for over a decade. How the cane had landed in Chicago the very day Smokey had turned up on Artemus's doorstep and they had both met Callie and Drake for the first time. How Karl had fashioned a gun that could kill demons months before his own death at their hands. How he and Drake had come by their weapons when they were six.

And now we have the mystery of Yashiro Kuroda, the bracelet, and the missing shop. Someone or something is behind this.

He recalled what Callie had said about the cane when he'd first met her. Ronald Stone had told her an angel had instructed him to have Callie sell it at Elton's auction house in Chicago after his death.

Artemus clenched his jaw.

If there is such an angel, I'm going to kick his ass if I meet him one day.

It wasn't long before they pulled off the highway and turned into the Fashion District. They parked a couple of blocks from the abandoned hotel and stepped out into the cool, night air. Even though the hour was late, there were still a few stragglers about.

A group of dark-clad men and women crossed the road and approached them.

"Hi, Isaac," Elton murmured. "Thanks for coming."

The head of the L.A. Vatican group studied them with a guarded expression. "So, why are we here again?"

"The Vatican was right," Artemus said. "We think there really *is* a gate to Hell in that hotel."

Isaac stared at him. Understanding dawned on his face. It was followed by disbelief.

"Wait. Are you saying you want us to go back in there?"

He pointed at the dark shape of the building looming in the night sky to the east.

"Yeah," Artemus replied.

"You're crazy!" Isaac snapped. "It's a demon den!"

"Relax," Serena said. "You have us."

She indicated their group.

Isaac scowled. "Is that supposed to make me feel better, somehow?"

Callie shrugged. "Yeah."

"By the way, did you find out who owned the place?" Drake asked Isaac.

The man sighed and rubbed the back of his neck, his expression still disgruntled. "It was recently bought by a conglomerate called Leviathan. The same name that was on the van we saw this morning."

A muscle jumped in Haruki's jawline. "Whoever owns Leviathan stole and falsified the deeds to that hotel. It was my brother Yashiro who purchased the building and the land it stands on before his trip to Hong Kong." Anger darkened his eyes. "It's the piece of real estate Tian Gao told my brother he was interested in buying the day he killed him."

Isaac frowned. "The CEO of Leviathan is a man called Daniel Delacourt." He paused at their startled expressions. "What, you know him?"

"Yes." Callie scowled. "He's the guy who tried to get me to join Ba'al."

"He's also after Haruki and his sword," Drake added in a hard voice. "We met Delacourt a few hours ago, in Hollywood Hills. And when I say 'met,' I mean we fought his demons."

One of the Vatican agents drew a sharp breath.

"Wait," the woman said. "You mean the crazy shit that

went down at that A-list Hollywood party tonight? The one that's all over the news right now? That was you?!"

"Yeah," Nate murmured.

Artemus turned and gazed at the hotel, more determined than ever. "Let's get this over with."

Elton put a hand on his arm. "Are you sure we can handle this? Maybe we should wait for backup."

Artemus shook his head stiffly. "We're running out of time." He glanced at Drake, Callie, and Smokey before studying Haruki with a thoughtful frown. "We should be able to handle them in our full forms. Besides, they won't be expecting us."

"By the way, I still haven't heard an explanation about those swords we saw this morning," Isaac reproached.

Elton sighed. "It's a long story."

Artemus waited impatiently while Elton, Isaac, and the Vatican agents armed themselves with dozens of silver-leaded-bullet magazines before leading the way toward the sewer entrance they'd used to break into the hotel that morning. They were about three hundred feet from the building when he slowed, puzzled by what he was sensing.

Or not sensing in this case.

"You feel it too?" Drake murmured.

"Yeah," Artemus said.

"What is it?" Serena asked.

Smokey's eyes glinted with a red light as he sniffed the air.

Callie stared at the hotel. "There's nobody home."

CHAPTER TWENTY-EIGHT

UNEASE FILLED HARUKI WHEN HE STEPPED INSIDE THE lobby of the hotel. The events that had taken place the last time he'd been there were still starkly fresh in his mind.

Still, a lot of even weirder shit has gone down since this morning.

Guilt stabbed through him at the thought of his father. He knew his old man was unlikely to forgive him for running away from home and breaking his promise not to contact Liao.

"Are you sure there are no demons about?" Ogawa asked in a low voice laced with tension.

"They'd be all over us by now if there were," Artemus replied.

Ogawa did not appear reassured by these words. Their footsteps echoed on the mosaic tiles as they gathered in the middle of the foyer.

"So, what do we do now?" Elton said.

Artemus switched a flashlight on. "We start looking for something that might be a gate to Hell." He paused and looked at Smokey, Drake, Callie, and Haruki. "This might go faster if we split everyone up in groups and one of us goes with each team. I think we'll be able to sense it if we're close to it."

"I agree," Drake said.

Haruki ended up on the first floor with Ogawa, Serena, Isabelle, and a Vatican agent. They headed down the hallway he'd passed through that morning with the body-guard and their men and entered one of the grand reception rooms.

"Looks like those guys weren't taking any chances." Serena frowned faintly at the faded marks on the floor and walls revealed in the light of their flashlights as they started exploring the disused space. "There's quite a lot of stuff missing."

"There's a good chance some of it was already gone," Isabelle said. "Don't forget this building is old. Looters might have been through the place years ago."

Serena looked over at Haruki after they completed a circuit of the room. "So, you got anything yet?"

"I'm not even sure what it is I'm supposed to be looking out for," Haruki muttered.

They crossed the corridor to inspect the second grand reception and found it to be just as bereft of anything that looked remotely gate-like. It was when they stepped inside the dining hall that Haruki felt something odd. He paused on the threshold of the dim space and blinked when the hairs rose on the back of his neck.

The beast inside him stirred.

"What is it?" Ogawa asked guardedly, his gaze on the shadows before them.

"I—" Haruki stopped, unsure how to voice the peculiar

sensation twisting through him. "I don't know. I just feel— weird all of a sudden."

Serena frowned. "Then, there's something here."

By the time Isabelle went to fetch the others, Haruki found himself standing in front of a large, marble fireplace at the other end of the chamber, his gaze riveted to the pale, rectangular imprint above it. His feet had carried him across the floor without conscious volition, as if he were in a dream. For a moment, he'd even forgotten about the other people around him.

The beast was fully awake now and gazing out of his body through the windows of his eyes, his heartbeat strong and steady above Haruki's racing pulse.

Someone came and stood next to him.

"Is this it?" Artemus said quietly.

Haruki hesitated before raising a hand and touching the faded wallpaper. The eyes of the dragon on the bracelet flared with a crimson light.

Suffocating doom swamped Haruki. He swayed where he stood, overwhelmed by the oppressive pressure bearing down on his very soul. The beast growled in agitation.

Artemus took hold of Haruki's arm and forced him to break contact with the wall. "Easy there."

Haruki swallowed down the bile rising in his throat, grateful for the other man's warm touch. His own skin felt like ice and he couldn't stop the shivers racing through him.

"Evil," he mumbled hoarsely. He looked blindly at Artemus, finally able to put a name to the sickening feeling threatening to drown him. "Whatever was here, it was evil."

Artemus's face hardened as he looked from Haruki to the pale imprint above the fireplace.

"I can sense it faintly," he murmured.

"Does that mean Ba'al already have the gate?" Elton asked stiffly.

It was Callie who replied.

"No." She studied Haruki's pale face with a concerned look. "If that were the case, I think we'd know by now. And they would never have let Haruki go earlier tonight."

"So, if Ba'al haven't got it and it isn't here, then where the hell is it?" Serena said.

"What do you mean, it's not at the hotel?" Tian Gao scowled. "Then, why have we been searching for the damn thing for the last two weeks?"

Delacourt poured himself a drink from the bar and headed over to the glass wall overlooking the mansion's gardens.

"The reason I know the gate is no longer there is because of what happened when Haruki Kuroda entered the place this morning," he drawled. "Or, to be more precise, what didn't happen. Had it been in the vicinity, the presence of its Guardian and its key would have triggered the gate off. That, my friend, would have alerted every demon in a ten-mile radius of the place."

Reluctant understanding dawned on Tian Gao's face.

"Is the attraction between a gate and its Guardian and key that powerful?" the Triad gang leader said gruffly.

Delacourt smiled faintly at the man's reflection in the glass. "You have no idea."

"So, what do we do now?" Tian Gao said, disgruntled.

Delacourt took a leisurely sip of his drink and turned to look at the Triad leader. "There is more than one way to skin a cat. Haruki Kuroda's awakening means that he and his new friends will be trying to find the gate too. So, we wait and we watch."

Tian Gao arched an eyebrow. "What, you think they'll just hand the thing over to us?"

Delacourt's smile widened. "I'm sure they could be... persuaded to."

Despite Ba'al's disastrous encounter with Artemus Steele and his group a few hours ago, he couldn't contain the thrill coursing through him. Or, more precisely, flowing through the demon inside him.

Over the years, as he and the creature who had taken over his soul when he was twenty had gotten to know one another, Delacourt had caught glimpses of the demon's distant past. They were memories from a time long gone, when the angels who would become the Grigori had not yet fallen and were still favored by God and Heaven. And they offered Delacourt a surprising window into the mind of the demon who lived and breathed beneath his skin.

Sometimes, in his dreams, Delacourt would see flashes of the epic battle that had taken place between the army led by the Archangel Michael and the one headed by Satan and the other leaders of the Fallen Watchers. A battle that had scorched the Heavens as well as the Earth for days on end. On those nights, Delacourt would often awaken with tears on his face and his heart heavy with a deep sense of loss. For the Grigori had been deprived of more than just the right to live in Heaven and bask in the divine light of God's existence following that fateful war. They had also lost their brothers in arms. Other angels and divine beasts who had stood by them for eons had turned against them in the blink of an eye, their will forged in the fires of righteousness and their actions guided by the One who had created them.

For a long time, the Fallen Watchers were overcome by profound sorrow, adrift in everlasting darkness and the fires of Hell. But loss and sadness soon burgeoned into rage and blame. And the ones who fell, the ones whose pale wings became as black as night and whose once exquisite heavenly bodies transformed into twisted monstrosities that repulsed all of God's creatures, the ones who would be called demons and Grigori, came to hate the beings they once called brothers, and God himself. And they swore vengeance. Vengeance that would see them rid the Earth of everything loved by God and his faithful servants. Vengeance that would see them destroy the comrades who once fought by their side. Vengeance that would see the entire world wallow in the same grief they had lived with for an eternity.

Delacourt knew why the demon inside him was so excited at the prospect of facing Artemus Steele and his companions. Because, unlike the last time the Watchers fought the divine beings and beasts who cast them into Hell, this time, it would be they who would be triumphant.

CHAPTER TWENTY-NINE

SERENA PERCHED ON THE EDGE OF A CHAIR AND TUGGED her jacket around her as she watched the lightening sky to the east. Day was breaking across the West Coast. Soon, the night chill would dissipate and L.A. would be awash with glorious sunshine once more.

Serena loved the sun. Maybe it was because she had been born in darkness and had grown up in the artificial twilight that permeated the life pods she and the other super soldier children had been locked in since their conception. She recalled the first time she, Nate, and Ben had witnessed their first sunny day shortly after their rescue, back at their adoptive father's estate. They'd sat outside for hours, marveling at how warm the rays of golden light felt on their skin and how beautiful the world looked bathed in it. And the one who had welcomed them into his home and his heart had watched on quietly, a sad smile on his face.

Pain and regret stabbed through Serena at the thought of the man they had abandoned the night she, Nate, and Ben had fled the estate, all those years ago. She knew their actions had hurt him and that he likely still lived with the grief of losing them. The fact that he had never come after them told Serena he understood in part the reasons why they had chosen to leave him and the world of the Immortals behind.

"Can't sleep?" someone murmured behind her.

Serena looked over her shoulder and saw Drake appear in the half-gloom. He was barefoot and wearing a loose T-shirt and sweatpants.

"No," she replied in a neutral voice, ignoring the butterflies that burst through her stomach at his presence.

She could no longer deny her attraction to Drake. On a purely physical level, she knew she wanted the man. And every time they were alone, like now, that fact became more and more undeniable.

Still, it doesn't mean I'm going to do anything about it.

Drake leaned wordlessly against one of the veranda's alabaster columns and watched dawn rise across the city, his expression inscrutable. Serena couldn't help but feel that the man's own demons had kept him awake too. He glanced at her when she rolled her sleeve back and tapped her smartband.

"Isn't it a bit early for a call?" he said, arching an eyebrow.

"Not where these guys are," Serena murmured.

She dialed the number Lou had given her and waited. The mercenary picked up on the second ring.

"Hey. What's up?"

Serena gazed at the sun where it finally peeked above the skyline. "I need a favor."

"Shoot."

～

HARUKI STARED AT SERENA. "YOU SPOKE TO SASAKI?"

It was just gone eight and they were having a hasty breakfast before convening with Isaac and his team to debate their next course of action.

"Yes," Serena said. "I'd been thinking about the hotel and all those missing objects. And I got a hunch. So, I asked Sasaki if Yashiro had investigated the building's contents after he purchased it."

Artemus put his coffee down, his expression keen. "And?"

"And I was right. Yashiro Kuroda had a number of items removed from the place the week before his death."

Surprise widened Haruki's eyes.

"Sasaki said Yashiro wanted them valued for insurance purposes, so he sent them to several antique valuers across the city," Serena explained.

Silence fell across the kitchen.

"I don't understand," Haruki finally said. He frowned faintly. "My brother could have had that done on site by an insurance company. Why did he feel the need to have them taken away?"

"Whatever your brother's reason was, be thankful for it," Drake said. "He unconsciously did you a favor."

"Yes," Callie murmured. "If you had entered that hotel when the gate was still inside, Ba'al would never have allowed you to leave the place. Not alive, anyway."

Haruki sobered at that.

Elton's expression turned thoughtful. "You know, this might explain what Isaac and his team observed."

Artemus stared at him, puzzled.

Understanding washed across Isabelle's face.

"You mean the demonic manifestations suddenly stopping two weeks ago?" the Immortal said.

Artemus blinked. "Oh. You're right."

"What do you mean?" Haruki said.

Elton related what had brought them to L.A. and what Isaac and his agents had discovered when they started investigating the recent spike in demon sightings in the city.

"Elton is saying the reason so many demons awakened in L.A. in the last month is because Yashiro brought the bracelet to the city," Artemus explained. "Seeing as the gate was in a building above ground, it must have resonated with the key even from a distance and attracted new demons to the area."

"And when the gate was moved out of the bracelet's range, the demonic manifestations ceased," Drake muttered. "Makes sense."

"Was there an inventory?" Callie looked at Serena. "Did Sasaki say whether Yashiro had a made a list of the items he sent away?"

Serena smiled. "Funny you should ask."

THE OFFICES OF THE KURODA GROUP LAW AND Accountancy firm were located in a three-story building, on an industrial estate in East L.A. The place backed onto an abandoned railway line half a mile west of Bristow Park and was flanked by two warehouses.

Artemus's heart sank as he studied the SUVs parked in front of the building and the dark-suited men guarding its entrance from where he sat in a car some hundred feet up the road.

"Well, it's not as if it's unexpected," Drake said. "Haruki's father would undoubtedly have increased the security measures around his businesses after his son's murder."

Artemus sighed. Drake was right.

It's a good thing we left Haruki and Ogawa with Callie and Smokey in Holmby Hills.

From what Sasaki had told Serena when she'd spoken to him that morning, the inventory of the items Yashiro Kuroda had sent away for valuation was sitting in the lawyer's desk drawer along with the receipts, in his office on the second floor.

"We could storm the place, but I don't think the kid would appreciate it if we knocked his men about," Drake said with a grimace.

"He'll bitch about it for days, that's for sure," Serena muttered from the driver's seat.

"We need a diversion," Nate stated next to her.

CHAPTER THIRTY

DRAKE HEADED UP THE LAST FLIGHT OF STAIRS AND opened the fire escape door at the top. A cool breeze washed over him when he stepped out onto the roof of the warehouse he and Serena had just snuck into. She came through behind him.

"This is a stupid idea," Drake declared.

"No, it's not," Serena retorted.

She headed south across the rooftop. Drake followed her reluctantly. They stopped at the edge of the building and studied the narrow alley separating them from the edifice housing the Kuroda Group offices.

Tires screeched in the distance behind them. A black sedan appeared at the end of the road. It accelerated before weaving wildly across the blacktop, as if the driver had lost control of the wheel.

The car drew abreast of the warehouse, took the wing mirror off one of the SUVs parked in front of the Kuroda Group building, and crashed into a fire hydrant fifteen feet from the main entrance. Water shot into the air from the burst mains and rained down onto the vehicle.

"That's like the oldest trick in the book," Drake muttered. "It's not gonna work. Those guards would have to be complete morons to fall—"

The Yakuza men rushed over to the sedan just as Artemus and Nate stepped out of the car and started arguing in loud voices.

"I believe that's our cue," Serena said smugly.

She took a few steps back, broke into a run, and cleared the alley in an easy jump. Drake scowled before following, landing atop the building seconds after her.

They made for the service exit at the other end of the roof. Serena slipped a suppressor onto her gun, shot through the lock, and carefully opened the metal door. A dim stairwell lit by emergency lights appeared beyond it. The sounds of Artemus and Nate's raised voices faded behind them as they started down the flight of stairs.

They stopped on the second-floor landing.

Serena signaled to Drake before carefully pulling the fire escape door open. He covered the gap with his gun while she slipped inside and stole through after her.

An empty hallway stretched out in front of them.

"Where to?" Drake murmured.

"His office is on the west side, right out back," Serena said in a low voice.

They moved silently down the passage, passed a janitor's closet, and came to an intersection. A low rumble of voices reached Drake's ears. He peered around the corner.

The commotion in front of the building had drawn people out of their offices and into what looked to be a large, administrative and secretarial pool room facing the road.

Drake motioned to Serena. They dropped into a low crouch, moved past the open doorway where the crowd had gathered, and turned into the adjacent corridor. Sasaki's office was at the end of the hall. Drake picked the lock on the door and sneaked inside with Serena.

The list and the receipts were where Sasaki had said they would be. Serena tucked the paperwork inside her jacket and followed Drake back out into the hallway.

They were halfway down the corridor when a woman stepped into the passage from a restroom. Drake's heart sank.

Damn.

The woman froze when she saw them. She took a step back, her expression growing suspicious. "Who are you?"

"I'm sorry, we seem to be a bit lost," Serena replied with a friendly smile. "We're visiting someone in the building."

The woman's gaze shifted past them to Sasaki's door. Her eyes widened. She turned and bolted down the corridor.

"Well, I think our cover is blown," Drake muttered when her alarmed shouts reached them a second later.

They dashed down the hallway, turned the corner, and plowed through the shocked crowd coming out of the front office. They made it to the fire escape and were halfway down the stairs when the first guards appeared in their path.

Serena grabbed the wrist of the guy aiming his gun at them, twisted it until he grunted and let go of the weapon, and front kicked him into the men at his back. Admiration shot through Drake as she brought the next three guys down in a matter of seconds, her body twisting fluidly through the air as she used the wall and the banister to deliver a series of swift roundhouse kicks to their heads. He knocked the gun out of the hand of the guard who came storming down the stairs from the second floor, punched the man in the jaw, and headed after Serena as she made for the door at the bottom of the stairwell.

They came out into a backyard adjoining the abandoned railway line just as a black SUV stormed around the side of the building. It screamed to a stop in a cloud of dirt some dozen feet from them. The back door flew open.

"Get in!" Artemus shouted from the front passenger seat.

Bullets peppered the ground in Drake and Serena's wake as they sprinted for the vehicle. They dove inside the SUV a second before Nate stepped on the accelerator and pulled away in a squeal of tires, Drake landing heavily atop Serena.

"Sorry," he mumbled, rolling off her.

Serena avoided his gaze and straightened in the back seat.

She looked over her shoulder. "Isn't this one of their cars?"

The Yakuza guards were standing outside the rear of their building, their faces dark with anger as they watched the SUV drive away.

"Well, we didn't exactly plan for a get-away vehicle," Artemus muttered, gazing at the fading figures in the wing mirror.

Drake pulled a face. "The kid's gonna be so pissed."

CHAPTER THIRTY-ONE

HARUKI NARROWED HIS EYES. "DID ANYONE GET HURT?"

"It's nothing they won't recover from," Serena replied blithely.

"A broken jaw and a cracked skull sound pretty damn serious to me, lady," Ogawa grumbled.

"Like I said, nothing they won't recover from," Serena repeated without a trace of remorse.

They were gathered in the kitchen of Callie's friends' mansion in Holmby Hills.

Haruki frowned at his bodyguard. "By the way, I've been meaning to ask you. How come you know all this stuff already?"

"I may have disobeyed your father's orders when I left the estate with you, but I'm still the head of security for the Kuroda Group," Ogawa said with a grunt. "I've been kept in the loop by one of the guys who came to Chicago with us." He paused. "Everyone's worried about you."

Haruki blinked, surprised. "They are?"

"Well, yeah," Ogawa muttered. "You're our future boss, after all."

Artemus rolled out a map of L.A. and the West Coast on the marble island in the middle of the room. From Sasaki's list, they now knew that thirty items had been removed from the abandoned hotel downtown and sent to various valuers across L.A. and its surrounding cities and towns by Yashiro Kuroda in the days preceding his death.

Of those items, twelve were too small to have been mounted above the fireplace in the dining hall where Haruki had sensed the gate. Which left them with eighteen antiques to check out over a sixty-mile radius.

"We should split up, like we did back at the hotel," Artemus said, studying the map with a thoughtful expression. "Only Drake, Callie, Haruki, Smokey, and I will be able to detect if any of these items are possible gates."

"You got addresses for all these places?" Elton said.

"Yeah." Lines furrowed Artemus's brow. "It would be best if we divide the area up equally. We have a lot of ground to cover."

Callie stepped out of the SUV with Nate and slammed the door of the vehicle shut behind her. She observed the building they'd parked across from with a guarded stare.

"What is it?" Nate said.

Callie looked around the rundown area of South L.A. they'd driven into. It was mid-afternoon and the place was almost deserted.

"It still puzzles me why Yashiro chose to send those antiques to so many different appraisers." She frowned faintly. "This is the third one we've been to so far and they're all the same. None of them are renowned auction houses. They're all obscure places in the middle of nowhere."

"Maybe it's the same reason you ended up bringing the cane to Chicago instead of taking it to an auction house in Philadelphia," Nate said.

Callie blinked at that. She mulled the super soldier's words over as they crossed the road and headed for the antique shop they'd come to visit. A bell chimed above their heads when Nate pushed the door open.

A woman looked up from behind a counter protected by a bulletproof-glass partition. "Hi. May I help you?"

"I phoned a short while back," Callie said. "I'm here to collect the item my employer left with you a couple of weeks ago."

"Oh, yes," the woman murmured. "Do you have the receipt?"

Callie handed the paperwork over. The woman perused the contents before disappearing through a door behind her. She returned a short while later with a large, rectangular item carefully wrapped in brown paper.

"We valued the painting at five thousand dollars." The woman opened a security door to the left of the counter and passed the package to them. "If you would like us to find your employer a buyer, we would be more than happy to do so."

Callie took the antique off her, her pulse thumping.

～

DRAKE, ELTON, AND MARK NAVIGATED AN ALLEYWAY close to an antique mall in Pasadena, about a mile east of Caltech.

"That must be it," Elton said, indicating a narrow, two-story building coming up on their right.

They slowed and stopped before the shabby frontage.

"Is this place even open for business?" Drake muttered.

He framed his face with his hands to block out the glare from the sun and peered through the dirty window of the shop.

"Sign on the front says it is," Mark said.

The door creaked loudly when they opened it. Drake stepped inside with the two Vatican agents and blinked as his eyes adjusted to the gloomy interior.

"Are we sure we have the right shop?" Elton said warily.

A grimace of distaste crossed his face when the shop's contents finally registered on his radar.

"Christ," Mark muttered. "This is a taxidermist's wet dream."

The place was a junkyard of dusty bric-a-brac, moth-eaten boxes housing old CDs and music records, and about a hundred stuffed animals. Drake looked uneasily at the beady eyes staring at them from all around the crowded shop and nearly missed the figure who was watching them silently from where he sat mounting a rabbit on a resin mannequin to their right.

"May I help you?" the apparition said in a lifeless voice.

The man was thin and gaunt, the shadows under his eyes so stark they rendered him an almost cadaverous appearance.

"We're here to see about an item our employer left with you a while back for valuation," Drake said.

The man studied him for a moment, put his scalpel down, and wiped his hands on his work apron as he rose to his feet. "Do you have the invoice?"

"Sure."

Drake gave him the copy. The man headed over to a tired-looking filing cabinet, rifled through the contents of a drawer, and removed a folder stuffed with documents. He took out a list and cross-referenced it with the receipt, the dirty nail of his forefinger scraping gratingly down the paper.

"Ah. The painting."

He turned and went through a door at the back of the shop.

"Is he a demon?" Elton hissed once the man was out of earshot.

Drake sighed. "No, he isn't."

"You sure?" Elton muttered. "'Cause this guy and his shop are giving me the heebie-jeebies."

"I feel you," Mark mumbled, staring at the stuffed bear towering over him.

The shop owner came back, a painting in hand.

Drake's pulse spiked as he stared at the gilded frame the man was holding and the beautiful, oil canvas landscape within it.

CHAPTER THIRTY-TWO

Serena crossed the intersection briskly, aware of the curious stares that followed her passage.

"Look, I'm not happy about this either," she murmured to the incensed rabbit in her arms. "Artemus didn't bring your leash and I would look like a negligent owner if I let you hop all over the place on a busy strip. Carrying a hellhound around as if he's a cute puppy is not my idea of fun."

Smokey bristled in her hold, his claws scoring marks across her leather jacket. Serena grimaced, checked out the buildings on the road she'd just entered in south Santa Monica, and spotted the frontage she was looking for. By the time she made it to the antique shop, three women had stopped her and asked if their kids could pet the rabbit.

Though Smokey stayed still and allowed the flurry of little hands to stroke his fur, Serena could tell he was minutes away from blowing a fuse and transforming into full hellhound mode, children be damned. The super soldier bit back a sigh.

Was he always this grouchy or is this Artemus's influence?

The shop they entered was similar to the two they'd already visited. Small and tacky, it seemed an odd place indeed for Yashiro Kuroda to have selected as a valuation venue. The woman behind the counter took the tab Serena gave to her and headed into a private office at the back to fetch the item the Yakuza heir had left in her care.

"What do you reckon?" Serena murmured to Smokey. "Third time lucky?"

Smokey gave her a look equivalent to a shrug. From the rabbit's reaction in the shops they'd visited earlier, the super soldier was pretty confident that neither of the two paintings sitting in the trunk of their car was a gate to Hell.

The hellhound's nose twitched when the shop owner reappeared with a package. Serena tensed.

ARTEMUS DRUMMED THE FINGERS OF HIS RIGHT HAND ON the polished, walnut desk.

"Will you stop that?" Isabelle hissed. "You're making me nervous. It's bad enough that this place looks like the freakin' Ritz."

She looked uneasily around the elegant room they were sitting in.

The auction house they'd called upon in Downtown Anaheim was located on the tenth floor of a highrise. It was a world apart from the seedy places they'd visited that morning in their hunt for the gate.

A man in a suit entered the waiting room through a side door.

"The paperwork is in order," he said smoothly, taking

the seat on the other side of the table. He passed the receipt Artemus had given him over. "My assistant is fetching the item from our vault as we speak."

"This is a nice place you have here," Isabelle murmured, eyeing the expensive furnishings in the room.

"Thank you." The man gazed at Artemus. "I'm surprised Mr. Kuroda chose our auction house to get the painting valued, when he already knew one of the best appraisers in the world."

Artemus gazed at him steadily. "Do we know each other?"

The man smiled and shook his head lightly. "I'm afraid not. Your reputation precedes you, Mr. Steele."

The door opened once more. A woman came in with a carefully wrapped package. Artemus stiffened when she handed it to the man.

He rose from behind the desk and carefully unveiled the painting.

"It's a replica, unfortunately," he murmured. "As you well know, an original Tintoretto would have sold for a substantial amount of money."

Artemus stared at the portrait the man had revealed.

OGAWA PULLED UP IN FRONT OF A ONE-STORY BUILDING covered in stucco.

Haruki stepped out of the car with the bodyguard and stared at the Ionic columns and terracotta architrave adorning the unusual frontage before them.

"Well, that's not something you see every day," Ogawa muttered.

The last antique shop on their list was in Santa Ana.

After the two establishments they had already visited, Haruki had expected the third place to be a dump too. Instead, it looked to be a historic property that once housed one of the city's first banks.

They pushed through the double oak doors framed by the columns, crossed a narrow marble anteroom, and entered a well-preserved banking hall that was now home to some dozen display cabinets.

The beast inside Haruki blinked one eye open.

"Can I help you?" someone said in a frail voice.

They turned and spotted a short, elderly man with rheumy eyes seated at a pedestal desk behind the refurbished teller's counter.

"Hi." Haruki swallowed past the sudden lump in his throat. "My brother had an item sent to you a while ago for a valuation."

Ogawa glanced at him curiously.

Haruki's pulse pounded in his veins as the old man rose unsteadily from his chair and came over to them. He recognized the sickening feeling forming in the pit of his stomach and raising the hairs on his nape, as did the creature inside him.

There's something here. Something demonic.

"Do you have the receipt?" the shop owner asked with a warm smile.

Haruki ignored Ogawa's now troubled stare and gave the elderly man the invoice Serena and Drake had stolen from Sasaki's office that morning. He blinked when his fingers fleetingly touched parchment-like skin.

Whatever it was that was making his senses prickle with dread, it wasn't the shop owner.

The old man shuffled over to his desk, took a ledger from inside the top drawer, and brought it back to the counter. He opened it and perused the contents of a page.

"Oh." Surprise washed across the old man's face. He looked up at Haruki, his expression turning contrite. "If I had known you were coming, I would have kept the items."

Haruki's heart thumped painfully against his ribs. "What do you mean, items? There was more than one antique?"

"Yes," the old man explained. "I returned them to the address the owner gave me, this very morning. Although the strongbox has some value, I'm afraid I found the second item to be quite worthless."

A sudden intuition blasted through Haruki.

"What was the address my brother gave you?" he asked in an urgent tone.

The old man turned the ledger around so they could see the page he'd been looking at.

"This is it." He tapped the lined paper with a pale finger. "Right there."

Haruki's knees went weak when he saw the address Yashiro had given the antique shop owner.

CHAPTER THIRTY-THREE

AKIHITO KURODA FROWNED AT THE PAPERWORK IN front of him. The words swam before his eyes. He released an irritated sigh, pinched the bridge of his nose, and closed the file.

A picture on his desk drew his gaze when he leaned back in his seat. He studied the photograph inside the simple ebony frame with a faint smile.

It had been taken fourteen years ago, at Yashiro's high school graduation ceremony, when he was still living in Japan. Haruki stood next to his brother, his arms wrapped around the older boy's waist and his face beaming with a rare grin.

Akihito's smile faded as pain stabbed through his heart once more. He touched the photograph of his two sons lightly before fisting his hand.

As a shateigashira to one of the most powerful Yakuza syndicates in the world, he had made it his life's mission to always maintain his composure and the dignity afforded to him by his stature. It was a task most men would find impossible, especially when death was a constant threat in their daily lives and their loved ones were eternal targets for their enemies.

Death was something Akihito was used to. He'd lost his grandparents and parents at a young age and his older brother when he was just fifteen. It was Ishida Kanzaki, the heir to a notorious Yakuza group and Akihito's classmate in school, who had extended a hand to him in his darkest hours. Although Akihito was grateful for the life granted to him by the organization he had entered and the brotherhood he had joined, there was no denying that it was a highly dangerous existence.

Though he had loved them both, he had not cried at the funeral of his wife or that of his mistress. To do so would have been a sign of weakness, in his own eyes and those of the world he inhabited. But Yashiro's death had been something else.

For the first time in his life, Akihito had drowned in pure grief. And he had nearly succumbed to the fury and the all-consuming desire for vengeance that had gripped him for days after.

If not for Kanzaki's gentle words to him on the night the Kuroda Group learned of the murder of their heir, Akihito knew he would have declared war against the Triad and unleashed a blood bath on the streets of L.A.

"It is at times like these that it is best to step back from your thoughts and instincts," Kanzaki had said to him. "I am not asking you to forgive or forget what was done to you and yours, Akihito. It is just that retaliation will only bring you further loss and regret. The Triad will not sit by quietly if you attack them. Haruki is bound to become a target too if you spill the blood of their men unwisely. So, allay the storm in your heart, my friend. And know that I am with you, tonight and always."

A frown marred Akihito's brow. Over a day had passed since Haruki and Ogawa had disobeyed his explicit instructions and fled the estate. Qing Shan Liao had rung him late the night before and told him about Haruki coming to meet him at a party in Hollywood Hills. He'd also gone on to recount a most implausible tale, one that had left Akihito wondering if the head of the L.A. Triad had been drunk when he'd decided to make the call. They'd agreed to speak again today, after Liao had informed him that Tian Gao Lee was now officially an enemy of the Triad and that he would do his utmost to find him and deliver justice for his despicable actions.

Haruki's face danced before Akihito's eyes. Worry twisted his gut.

As his firstborn, it had always been Yashiro's fate to take over the Kuroda Group one day. It was a destiny Yashiro had been at peace with and a role that Akihito was confident he would have been great at. Though he had a kind and just heart, Yashiro had also been a keen and ruthless businessman and had shared Akihito and Ishida Kanzaki's visions of taking their syndicate in a different direction, one that would see them fully embrace the world of legitimate enterprise and slowly discard the ventures that had earned them a dark reputation for so long. It was the only way organizations like theirs would survive the future.

As for Haruki, it had been Akihito's intention to let his younger son live a life apart from the Yakuza if he chose to do so. And it had been clear to him for some time that that was exactly Haruki's wish.

Of his two sons, his youngest was the one with the more innocent and gentle heart, just like his mother. Although Akihito had originally promised his mistress he would leave Haruki's upbringing in her hands, her premature death had meant he had had to break that vow. Up till that point, Haruki's existence had only been a rumor in the Yakuza world and he had not yet become a potential target for the Kuroda Group's enemies.

All that had changed after his mother's death, when it was accidentally revealed that he was Akihito Kuroda's son and potential heir. To leave Haruki without the protection of the Kuroda Group after that would have been a death warrant for the boy.

And so, Akihito had been forced to bring the child into his dark and dirty world. And he had done so while deliberately avoiding showing him any affection, just as he had done with Yashiro.

Though he loved both his sons more than his own life, Akihito knew that any overt signs of fondness for his flesh and blood would make his enemies more greedy and likely to hurt them to get to him.

Akihito had actually been relieved when Haruki started to rebel. For a time, he had thought he had killed the boy's vivacious spirit by forcing him to leave his grandparents' home. But Haruki had only grown more mutinous and strong-spirited as the years went by.

It was Yashiro who had first told Akihito of Haruki's desire to go to Stanford to get a business degree. Though Akihito would have preferred it if the boy had chosen a university closer to home, he had still supported his decision, a fact that he knew had shocked his youngest son.

All of that was now immaterial. With Yashiro's death, Haruki had been forced into taking center stage and assuming the mantle of heir to the Kuroda Group. A role Akihito had never wished for him and which he had granted him with the greatest reluctance following a long debate with Ishida Kanzaki.

Akihito realized now that it had been foolish of him to expect Haruki's defiant nature to abate overnight. Although he knew the young man would be serious about the role that had befallen him, it appeared that he still needed to learn to control his instincts. That Renji Ogawa had also chosen to defy Akihito shocked him more.

It's because of Riuji. Those two were closer than beans in a pod. Akihito sighed. *Still, where the devil are you, Haruki?*

He rose from his seat and headed out of his study, resigned to taking a short walk around the estate to help clear his mind. His guest would soon be arriving and there would be much for them to discuss over dinner.

It was as he approached the mansion's main foyer that a commotion drew his attention. He stepped inside the elegant vestibule and saw the housekeeper directing two guards as they carried a wide metal box across the genkan and into the house.

"What is going on?" Akihito murmured.

The housekeeper startled and turned toward him.

"I'm so sorry, Kuroda-sama," she said, bowing respectfully. "This package just came. It is—" She paused and swallowed, a nervous expression washing across her face. "It is addressed to Yashiro-san."

Akihito stiffened. He stared from the housekeeper to the box, unease coiling through him.

"Open it," he ordered quietly.

The two guards carefully laid the casket on the ground and unlatched the iron clasps securing it. An object swathed in plastic packaging sat inside. The guards lifted the item out and removed the wrappings from around it.

Akihito blinked.

It was a large, gilded mirror.

"Sir, your guest has arrived."

Akihito startled. He looked up and saw Ogawa's right-hand man standing on the threshold of the mansion.

A concerned look flashed in the man's eyes. "Sir, are you okay?"

Akihito hesitated before dipping his chin. He didn't know why the arrival of a package for Yashiro had unnerved him so. And he couldn't explain the uncanny feeling growing inside him at the sight of the mirror now resting against the console table in his hallway.

The sensation was akin to being deep underwater. It was as if all light and sound were being sucked out of the room. And the air was becoming heavy too, so heavy Akihito could feel his lungs start to ache from the lack of oxygen.

What is this suffocating atmosphere?

Footsteps approached on the gravel path that led to the main entrance. Two guards escorted a group of men inside the genkan. At the head of the party was a tall, blond, brown-eyed figure.

"Kuroda-san," Daniel Delacourt murmured with a respectful bow of his head. "It is a pleasure to finally meet you. Thank you again for agreeing to see me. I'm sure the Kuroda Group and Leviathan will go on to build many successful business ventures together."

Akihito took a labored breath and forced himself to shake the hand the man proffered. Inexplicable dread exploded inside him when their skin made contact.

The other man's flesh was as cold as ice.

Delacourt's gaze shifted to the object resting against the table to his right. Akihito couldn't help but notice that all the men with Delacourt were staring unblinkingly at it too, their expressions almost...hungry.

"What a beautiful mirror," Delacourt said, his mouth curving in a smile.

CHAPTER THIRTY-FOUR

"SLOW DOWN!" OGAWA YELLED.

Haruki dropped gears, swerved around a line of cars, and stepped on the gas pedal, his stomach churning with trepidation.

They were on the San Diego Freeway, headed north toward Malibu. Ogawa had already tried calling the guards at the mansion but to no avail; no one was picking up. Which only intensified the fear growing inside Haruki.

He knew now that what he'd felt back at the antique shop in Santa Ana was a trace of the demonic energy projected by the gate. And if it had been that strong without even being there, then its aura would be even more overwhelming up close. Which meant the demons in L.A. would no doubt sense it too. Haruki gritted his teeth.

From what Ogawa had learned that morning after talking to one of the guards at the estate, Akihito Kuroda was having a guest over for dinner tonight to discuss business.

Don't die, old man! Yashiro would never forgive me!

Haruki's hands clenched on the steering wheel of the

car, a barrage of emotions nearly drowning him at the thought of losing his father. Anger, frustration, love, regret. All of it swirled around and through him in a violent maelstrom that made his heart pound painfully. But one emotion dominated all the others. He blinked, shocked at the sudden tears that blurred his vision.

And I wouldn't forgive myself either, you old bastard!

Ogawa's smartband chimed. His eyes widened at the number that flashed on the screen.

"I was just about to call you!" he said in a rush of words. "Master Haruki found the gate! It was in Santa Ana." Ogawa paused, a tense frown darkening his face as he listened to the voice coming through the wireless receiver in his ear. "No, we don't have it. The owner of the antique shop sent it away this morning." The bodyguard's Adam's Apple bobbed convulsively as he swallowed. "It's at the Kuroda estate, in Malibu." He paused before glancing at a sign up ahead. "We're coming up to Santa Monica now." A bark of cynical laughter escaped him next. "Tell him not to do anything stupid?" He looked at Haruki, frustration pasted across his face. "What do you think I've been doing for the last twenty minutes?! Just hurry!"

Ogawa ended the call and swore when Haruki overtook two cars and a tow-truck in a squeal of tires, sending him cannoning into the passenger door.

"Was that Artemus?" Haruki asked stiffly.

"Yes," Ogawa replied in a grim tone. "They're on their way."

Daylight was fading by the time they entered the hills north of Paradise Cove. They hit the dirt road that signaled the boundary of the private land that surrounded the estate and stormed up the slope. Coldness filled Haruki's veins as they skidded around a corner and he spied the unlit torches above the estate walls.

They're here!

The otemon gate was wide open when they drove up to it. Haruki flew through the entrance and down the paved driveway toward the dark, main house, his pulse thrumming wildly. He brought the car to a screeching halt in the forecourt where several SUVs stood parked and jumped out of the vehicle, only to gasp and stagger to a stop.

The demonic energy shrouding his home slammed into him like a wall and nearly brought him to his knees.

Haruki clenched his jaw and slowly straightened against the savage pressure bearing down on his body, his breaths coming in labored pants as he tried desperately to draw air into his lungs.

How the hell did I not sense this until now?!

Ogawa dropped onto his hands and knees beside him, sweat beading his face. He retched and threw up.

"Stay here!" Haruki barked at the bodyguard.

The juzu bracelet transformed into the flaming sword as he stepped onto the gravel path that led to the main doors of the mansion, the beast inside him writhing and twisting agitatedly in response to the foul forces washing across his skin. The air grew lighter as the creature's energy flowed through him and it became easier to move.

Haruki entered the genkan and stumbled to a stop when he saw the mutilated bodies of several guards and the housekeeper lying in pools of blood in the hallway. Despair filled him.

No! He can't be dead! Not him!

Haruki's knuckles whitened on the handle of the sword. He gritted his teeth and headed past the bloodied corpses, his feet taking him unerringly toward the concentration of demonic power he could sense at the rear of the mansion. He slid the double-paneled, wood-framed shoji doors open and froze. Icy fingers wrapped around his heart at the sight that met his eyes.

"Welcome, Guardian," Delacourt said.

The blond man stood behind Akihito Kuroda's seat, at the head of the airy, two-story chamber that opened onto a veranda overlooking an immense, traditional Japanese garden.

Tian Gao stood to Delacourt's right, a smirk on his demonic face.

Haruki studied the fiendish horde crowding the enormous space and the dead bodyguards on the tatami floor before zeroing in on his father's pale face. The latter sat semi-conscious and seemingly unharmed. Like a moth to a flame, Haruki's gaze finally found the source of the evil force pulsing through the room.

There, on the wall behind Delacourt and his father, was a large, gilded mirror. Just as he'd suspected, the artifact was a lot more potent up close than when he'd felt the remains of its presence in Santa Ana.

Akihito Kuroda's eyes fluttered open. He blinked, his pupils constricting as he focused on Haruki. "Haru—ki?"

Haruki's stomach clenched at his father's weak voice. That he was even conscious was a testament to the older man's strength and will power.

Panic filled Akihito Kuroda's face when he registered Haruki's presence, his glazed expression turning lucid for an instant. "No! *Run, son!*"

The head of the Kuroda Group struggled to his feet. Delacourt pressed a hand down on his shoulder, his nails extending into wicked talons that pierced the flesh beneath it and caused Akihito Kuroda to gasp and blanch.

Rage exploded inside Haruki when he saw blood bloom on his father's yukata.

He gripped his sword with both hands and bolted toward Delacourt, a red haze filling his vision.

"*Get your filthy hands off him!*"

A dark shape flashed in front of Haruki. Something that felt like a lead pipe smashed into his stomach. Air left him in a grunt. He stumbled back several steps and fell to one knee, the metallic taste of blood coating his tongue as he choked and wheezed.

"Let's have some fun, Guardian," Tian Gao said where he towered over him, the clawed fist he'd used to punch Haruki slowly uncurling as he lowered his arm to his side.

"Don't kill him," Delacourt ordered coolly. "The gate is not open yet."

Haruki looked past Tian Gao and saw fear fill his father's eyes.

CHAPTER THIRTY-FIVE

THE HAIRS ROSE ON ARTEMUS'S ARMS. HE STARED FROM the fine, blond strands standing on his skin to the storm clouds gathering above Malibu as Nate barreled down the Pacific Coast Highway.

Artemus clenched his teeth when he detected the demonic energy building up ahead of them. He'd first made it out when they were still near Long Beach.

"Shit." Serena frowned in the front passenger seat. "Even I can feel that. It's like someone's trying to squeeze my brain out of my skull."

"This is stronger than what we dealt with in New York," Drake said stiffly, his eyes flashing crimson for an instant.

Artemus glanced at his brother. He could sense the darkness inside Drake growing the closer they got to their destination. He could also feel him fighting back against the demon who had lived inside him and tormented him for over two decades.

Red lightning flashed in the center of the boiling, dark

mass in the night sky as the super soldier took the exit that led into the hills housing the Kuroda estate. Tires screeched behind them. The headlights of multiple SUVs washed through the rear windscreen of their vehicle.

Elton and his team were following them with the entire L.A. Vatican group in tow.

"Drake is right," Callie said in a voice filled with trepidation. "We need to hurry. Haruki is in trouble!"

Nate floored the gas pedal.

SHADOWS FILLED THE CHAMBER AROUND HARUKI. THE air shivered with thickening spirals of blackness. Demons materialized from the inky pools, their ethereal forms trembling before solidifying out of thin air. They stepped onto the straw mats, their hungry gazes moving from Haruki to the gilded mirror at the head of the room.

The antique throbbed where it sat on the wall, the gold frame and silver surface slowly darkening while ripples distorted its very structure.

Haruki staggered upright, his heart thudding in tandem with the foul pulsation echoing from the object. His eyesight altered, the gloom around him abating as it had done in the gardens in Hollywood Hills the night before.

Tian Gao's leg arced toward his chest. Haruki raised the sword and blocked the strike inches from his rib cage, his feet skidding backward across the floor. The demon grinned and threw a punch toward his head, deadly talons curving to shred his flesh.

Something glimmered on Haruki's face as he jumped

out of the way. Tian Gao's claws glanced off his left cheek a second later. Sparks erupted where the demon made contact with his skin.

His talons did not cut Haruki.

Surprise flashed in Tian Gao's yellow eyes.

"Leave him be," Delacourt said, faint excitement underscoring his voice. He stared from Haruki to the mirror. "He is starting to awaken. And so is the gate."

The demon's words made a cold pit of dread form in Haruki's stomach. He touched his face and felt small, hard plates under his fingertips. A burst of power surged through him from the mark on his back. More scales bloomed on his hands and arms. The beast within him was fully roused now, his life force an orange thread that twisted around Haruki's very soul.

Alarm filled Haruki.

Not enough. This is not enough power to defeat them all!

The beast's voice reached him through the blood pounding inside his skull. Though Haruki sensed the creature's fury at the presence of the mirror and the demons, his tone was cool and calm.

Get ready.

Sigils appeared on the flat of the flaming blade in Haruki's hand, strange lines and shapes that formed characters he neither recognized nor understood. They were brighter and more prominent than when he'd last seen them.

Haruki stared at them dazedly, conscious of a strange prickling on his head and back once more. Callie's words about the symbols being the key to opening the gate rose in his mind at the same time that a solid blotch of darkness appeared in the center of the mirror.

A feral grin distorted Delacourt's face when the sordid apparition expanded, corrupt tendrils tinged with crimson arcing across the dull surface before twisting and merging. Blackness rapidly filled the interior of the mirror. Delacourt's skin fluttered and trembled, the demon inside him finally emerging.

Haruki's eyes widened as he watched the man's body swell and transform into a monstrous shape.

Low growls rumbled out of Tian Gao and the other demons, their tawny eyes blazing with admiration and respect as they looked upon the true form of their commander.

A dim voice sounded in Haruki's ears above the rapid thumping of his pulse. He blinked in shock when he realized it was his own.

The beast was speaking through his mouth, his gravelly voice deep and resonant as he recited a holy incantation.

The first sigil on Haruki's sword flashed gold. It turned crimson a heartbeat later. Tremors started shaking the room. The blackness occupying the inside of the mirror swelled and spilled over the physical boundaries of the frame.

Haruki took a step back as the evil energy pouring off the antique doubled in intensity. Panic swarmed his consciousness.

No. Stop! You have to stop translating the sigils!

The beast spoke to him.

Stand your ground and be not afraid. It is almost done. And they are almost here. We are not alone, child.

The beast's placid tone filtered through Haruki and allayed the fear building inside him. Sweat beaded his forehead as his lips continued to frame words he did not know. Deep in the marrow of his soul, Haruki knew he could never disobey the beast. To do so would be to deny himself. And he could sense them now.

The ones whose life forces were akin to his. The ones who possessed the same divine power and will coursing through him.

The sword vibrated in Haruki's grip as more symbols glowed gold then red. Heat exploded inside his abdomen as he uttered the penultimate incantation. It multiplied and grew, filling his stomach and rising in his throat. Wisps of smoke curled from his nostrils and mouth. The prickling on his head and back intensified ten-fold. His tailbone started itching alarmingly.

Something tore through the clothes on his back, all the way down his spine and beyond. Tiny projections sprouted from the center of his scalp and poked through his hair. A pair of bony, silver stubs emerged from his mandibles and framed his scale-covered cheekbones and jawline. The skin stretched tight over his face as his skull structure altered to fit the beast within.

The final invocation tumbled from Haruki's lips.

The last symbol changed from gold to crimson.

Blinding light engulfed the sword in his hand. It thickened and lengthened, the blade turning the color of white gold while the flames engulfing it blazed scarlet. A scream tore out of his throat as power bloomed inside his very core. It expanded rapidly, a fiery energy that throbbed and pulsed with every beat of his heart and that of the beast within him.

The beast who had now fully awakened.

The dazzling brilliance that had swamped Haruki's senses abated. Sight and sound returned. With them finally came the knowledge of what he was. A savage thrill filled him then, his blood boiling as he faced the creatures he had been born to fight.

Haruki opened his mouth and inhaled deeply. His chest swelled to gargantuan proportions. The heat inside his stomach and throat intensified until it was a veritable inferno.

The Dragon roared out a river of fire.

CHAPTER THIRTY-SIX

Flames exploded from the mansion's rear rooftop as Nate braked to a halt in the forecourt. They jumped out of the vehicle, their weapons in hand. Serena cursed and dug her heels into the ground, bracing against the hellish energy battering the Kuroda home.

The demon inside Drake stirred behind its rigid prison, its foul power resonating with the demonic waves throbbing from the house. He caught Artemus's anxious glance and clenched his jaw before dipping his chin slightly. Relief danced in his brother's eyes.

The other SUVs screamed to a stop behind theirs.

Isaac stepped out of his vehicle with four Vatican agents and froze, his eyes widening. "What the—?"

The color drained from his face as he sagged down on one knee, the other agents falling to the ground behind him. Two of them started being violently ill.

"Damn." Sweat popped on Elton's forehead. He clung to the wing mirror of the SUV he'd just alighted from. "This pressure is—"

"Insane," Isabelle grunted.

She scowled and straightened, Mark and Shamus rising at her side with some difficulty. Elton and Isaac joined them a moment later.

Artemus glanced at the rest of the Vatican agents where they'd fallen beneath the savage, demonic power filling the air. "Looks like it's just gonna be us for the time being."

He released the sword inside his switchblade. Drake pulled his knife out of its sheath and unleashed his blade, his watch expanding into the shield that covered his left arm. Callie's cane grew into the scepter at the same time that she morphed into her full Chimera form, her eyes flashing jade. Smokey shook himself and swelled into his hellhound shape, a red light filling his eyes. Serena and Nate slammed their liquid-armor-suit discs onto their chests and depressed the switches that activated their battle gear.

Isaac's jaw dropped open as he stared at Callie and Smokey.

"I'll explain later," Elton told him. He glanced at Artemus and Drake. "About the wings too."

The Vatican agent's mouth opened and closed soundlessly.

"What wings?!" he finally spluttered.

They found Ogawa inside the mansion. The bodyguard had crawled past the dead bodies of several men and a woman and lay barely conscious in the entrance hall. He blinked when Artemus dropped down beside him and rolled him gently onto his side.

"Help him," Ogawa rasped. He indicated the end of the hallway with a trembling hand, where smoke wreathed the air and the orange glow of flames danced across the mansion's ebony floors and internal paper walls. "Help Master Haruki, please!"

Nate hefted Ogawa over his shoulder and headed back the way they'd come. "I'll take him outside."

Darkness seeped through Drake's soul as they followed the sounds of demons' screeches down the passage; the devil within him was growing stronger in the presence of its kin. He gritted his teeth and sought the thread of light entwined around his soul. The one that the unearthly female apparition he had met when he was at death's door several weeks past had granted him before his powers fully awakened.

The divine energy that balanced the evil half of him and grounded the monster he would soon become.

GOOSEBUMPS BROKE OUT ACROSS ARTEMUS'S SKIN AS heat flowed through his body from the marks on his back and his power surged.

An echo of the same energy pulsed inside him from the one who had just awakened. The one who, from the sounds of the fight they were approaching, was holding his own against a horde of demons.

Artemus walked through a wall of smoke and entered the battleground ahead of the others. He slowed to a stop, his gaze riveted to the creature taking center stage in the middle of a large, airy hall whose roof was currently on fire.

"Is that Haruki?" Serena said.

"Yes," Drake replied grimly. "And that—" He indicated a block of solid blackness visible above the demons crowding the chamber, "must be his gate."

Artemus glimpsed the dark doorway at the head of the room; it appeared to be sealed still.

"What is he?" Isabelle said in a cautious voice, her eyes on Haruki.

Artemus's gaze found the beast again. This time, he made out the name that danced through his consciousness. "He's the Colchian Dragon."

The silver dragon's claws anchored him to the ground as he carved through the wall of fiendish creatures with the flaming sword in his hands. The blade had changed too; it was bigger and paler than before, its flames now a rich red.

Talons scraped harmlessly down the scales on the beast's arms and back. He gored a demon with the deadly horns framing his face and battered the ones on his left with a powerful wave of his thick, spiky tail. Two creatures landed on his back and impaled themselves on the thick, silver barbs that extended from his spine.

The Dragon shook the bodies off him, threw his head back, and released a thunderous roar that shook the rafters. A jet of white-hot flames left his jaws and engulfed his attackers in the next instant. The demons caught in the fiery stream screamed and stumbled backward, their bodies glowing brightly before exploding into clouds of ash.

The Dragon looked over his shoulder when he sensed the presence of Artemus and the others. He scowled, his slit-like eyes flashing orange.

"About goddamn time!" Haruki growled. "Did you guys stop for a freaking picnic?!"

Artemus's fascination slowly faded. Lines furrowed his brow. "Well, if someone hadn't been in such a rush, we would have all arrived at the same time! Oh yeah, who was that moron again? Why, it was *you!*"

The spines on Haruki's head and back bristled. "You asshole! Did you just call me a moron?!"

Callie grinned, her eyes sparkling as she beheld their kin. Smokey huffed in pleasure and transformed into the ultimate, three-headed, golden-eyed Cerberus.

Isaac paled.

Haruki blinked at the hellhound's new shape. "Okay, that's all kinds of cool right there."

The air tore open with loud ripping noises that made Artemus's teeth vibrate. Dark rifts appeared in the smoke above their heads, the edges tinged with crimson. He tensed as demons of all sizes and shapes emerged from them, some with wings as wide as they were tall. The creatures gravitated toward the gate, their hungry gazes unblinking.

A thin, red line appeared at the top of the black doorway. It tore down the center seconds later.

"That's not good!" Drake said.

The crowd of demons shifted. An unconscious, elderly Asian man appeared behind the milling mass, body limp where he slouched in a chair. Artemus's pulse spiked as Delacourt and Tian Gao finally came into view.

"Crap," Isabelle muttered. "He's even bigger than that Park guy was."

"The taller they are, the harder they fall," Serena said, unsheathing her blades. Nate and Shamus stared at her. She grimaced at their expressions. "I mean the bad guys, obviously."

"Whatever happens, my father must not come to any harm," Haruki stated adamantly as they all gazed at the gigantic form of Delacourt's demon.

CHAPTER THIRTY-SEVEN

DELACOURT LOOKED OVER THE HEADS OF SOME HUNDRED demons to the group at the far end of the chamber. A feverish excitement gripped him when he beheld the three divine beasts and the two men he'd been waiting for.

He glanced dismissively at the other figures with them. "The gate is opening. We no longer need the Dragon." A vicious smile distorted his features. "Spare Drake Hunter. Kill the rest."

The demons turned as one, their yellow eyes focusing on the enemy in their midst. Tian Gao grinned and headed into the melee, his gaze on Haruki Kuroda.

~

"PLAYTIME'S OVER," DRAKE SAID IN A HARD VOICE.

He inhaled deeply and concentrated.

The walls he'd erected to contain the devil inside him appeared in his mind's eye. His pulse accelerated as he carefully lowered the shields.

A gasp left his throat when the demon emerged, its corrupt energy filling his body in a single heartbeat.

The marks on his back trembled before unfurling into black wings, the limbs shearing through his clothes. A black armor made of a metal not of this world materialized out of thin air and covered his body from the neck down. Flames appeared on his fingertips. They engulfed the weapon in his right hand, darkening and lengthening the blade to a broadsword as tall as him, its edges twisted into wicked teeth. The shield on his left arm grew dull before sprouting runes that glowed with a crimson light.

Bloodlust flooded Drake. The desire to slaughter everything and everyone in his path roared through his veins. He gritted his teeth, grasped the thread of light pulsing in his soul, and lassoed the demon with it.

The devil screamed. His screech of outrage and fury faded under the power of the divine ties that now bound him.

Drake breathed a sigh of relief when he felt his sanity return.

"You okay?" Artemus said beside him.

His brother had assumed his ultimate form, his snowy wings tucked against his back and his skin covered with a silver sheen where it was exposed beneath the golden armor he wore. Pale flames danced on the giant broadsword in his right hand.

Drake glanced at Smokey's anxious expression before staring into his brother's equally worried eyes. "Yes, I am."

"Was that what you meant by wings?" Isaac asked Elton leadenly.

"Way cool," Haruki muttered, his eyes glittering as he beheld them.

∼

SERENA DUCKED BENEATH A FLURRY OF TALONS, SLICED the throats of three demons, and grunted when two creatures barreled into her back and took her to the ground.

The liquid-armor suit deflected their claws as they sliced and gouged at her. She blocked the talons heading for her eyes with her forearms, kneed one of the demons in the groin, and arced her leg into a sweeping kick. Her right foot connected with the second demon's temple with a crack.

Nate shot the creatures in the back of the head. The demon above her shifted into his human shape before slumping onto her chest, his eyes growing dim.

Serena grimaced, rolled the body off her, and flipped onto her feet.

"That sight never gets old," Nate said.

She followed his gaze to the figures fighting the demons emerging from the rifts in space above them.

Drake and Artemus moved effortlessly through the creatures, their wings striking the air with loud thumps while their powerful blades turned the enemy into blazing figures that burst into clouds of ash.

"Twenty-one!" Artemus shouted as he stabbed a winged demon through the heart.

Drake scowled. "Twenty-three!"

He twisted through the air and carved the throats of two demons.

"Hey, that's cheating!" Artemus protested. "You can't do them two at a time!"

"Oh yeah?" Drake said. "Says who?"

"Are they actually keeping score?" Serena said dully.

"I said they were impressive," Nate mumbled. "I never said they were smart."

CALLIE RELEASED A SONIC ROAR THAT IMMOBILIZED three demons and threw the scepter. The weapon sang through the air, pierced the creatures' hearts, and curved before winging back toward her.

She closed her hand around it, blocked the strikes of two demons, and headbutted them in the face. The snakes on her head hissed and tore through the creatures' skin at the same time her horns gored their eyes. The demons screeched and tumbled back.

Smokey landed on top of them and finished them off with his powerful jaws.

The hellhound suddenly paused. He raised his three heads and gazed at two rifts floating some ten feet above them. A low growl rumbled out of his throats.

Callie tensed when she saw what emerged from the crimson portals.

"WHAT THE HELL ARE THOSE?" ARTEMUS SAID.

He stared at the grotesque apparitions that had just stepped out of the cracks in space close to Callie and Smokey.

The creatures were as big as Smokey and bore two heads each. Their deformed bodies were black as night, their limbs and spines crooked and twisted into strange angles. A foul, red light radiated from their eyes, while their gaping, misshapen jaws revealed vicious fangs.

"They kinda look like hellhounds," Drake muttered. "Butt-ugly hellhounds."

Smokey's eyes flashed gold as he glared at the newcomers.

"And I don't think our hellhound likes them," Drake added.

The tremors shaking the chamber intensified.

Artemus's gaze shifted to the gate at the head of the room. The red crack splitting its center was thickening, the darkness around it boiling as if it were alive.

"We need to shut that thing down!"

"Yeah, well, technically, the only one who can do that is Haruki," Drake said.

Artemus narrowed his eyes at the Dragon where the latter fought a group of demons.

His grip tightened on the broadsword in his right hand. "Let's clear a path for him then, shall we?"

HARUKI FOUND HIS FATHER ON THE VERANDA.

Akihito Kuroda had managed to crawl outside the chamber before exhaustion took over, the demons in the room evidently too engaged in their battle with Artemus and the others to bother killing him yet.

Haruki dropped down beside the older man and rolled him gently onto his back before lifting him in his arms and carrying him into the gardens.

Akihito Kuroda's eyes fluttered open when the cool night air struck his face. His pupils widened.

"Haruki?" he said hoarsely. "Is that really you, son?"

Haruki lowered his father gently onto the grass and propped him up against a tree.

He straightened and met the older man's gaze unflinchingly. "Yes, it is."

"So, that's where you're hiding, you little rat!" someone growled behind him.

Haruki turned and beheld Tian Gao. The demon was crossing the grounds toward them, his huge shape backlit by the flames ripping through the mansion's rooftop.

Tian Gao stopped a few feet away. He stared from Haruki to Akihito Kuroda before grinning savagely.

"This is perfect!" A bark of guttural laughter escaped him. "Not only did I kill your firstborn, I now get to slaughter you and your bastard runt!"

Cold fury filled Haruki at the demon's words.

"Haruki?" Akihito Kuroda said quietly.

"Yes, father?" Haruki murmured in a steely voice.

"Show him no mercy."

The Dragon shuddered at the command. He reached inside himself and drew on all the power of the beast living under his skin. A holy light erupted from his core and filled his entire body. His scales and horns shifted from silver to gold. He dug his heels into the grass and gripped the fiery broadsword in both hands.

"Let's dance, asshole," the Dragon growled at the demon.

CHAPTER THIRTY-EIGHT

BLOOD DRIPPED INTO CALLIE'S LEFT EYE FROM THE GASH on her forehead. She panted and deflected the claws headed for her gut a hairbreadth from her body.

The monster before her snarled and snapped his jaws at her neck. The snake at the base of her spine countered with vicious headbutts while the ones on her head sank their fangs into the creature's faces.

The demon hellhound cried out and jumped back five feet. Rage filled its crimson eyes. It lowered its heads and charged at her.

Callie slammed the scepter on the ground and jumped, using the weapon as an anchor and pivoting her body through the air. Her clawed feet slammed into the beast's chest and sent him staggering to the side.

Smokey landed beside her, acid drool dripping from the jaws of his middle head where it was locked on the second demon hellhound's shoulder. The creature growled and scored Smokey's flanks with his claws. Smokey winced and held on grimly.

DRAKE IMPALED A DEMON THROUGH THE HEART AND tore his sword out of the creature's body seconds before it burst into flames and ash. He blocked the talon heading for his temple with his shield, kicked the demon hurtling toward him in the chest, and decapitated the one on his left.

Supersonic booms echoed around him as Artemus flashed through the air and disposed of the demons in his path, ash filling the air in the wake of his passage.

They'd sealed most of the rifts while they were cutting down the demonic army that had invaded the mansion. There were less than a hundred of the creatures left and Serena and the others were shrinking that number even as he watched.

Drake turned to the wall of throbbing darkness at the head of the room. The red line in the center had thickened and now occupied a third of the gate's width. He knew instinctively that once it filled the doorway, the portal would finally open and Hell would descend on Earth.

Artemus appeared beside him. They studied Delacourt's demonic figure where he stood before the gate, his yellow gaze focused unblinkingly on them.

"It's like he's waiting for us," Drake murmured.

Artemus frowned. "Let's go say hi."

TIAN GAO SLAMMED HIS PALMS ON THE FLAT SIDES OF the broadsword an inch from his head. He grimaced when the fire singed his skin. Black blood pooled out of the wound on his left flank as he grunted and pushed back against his attacker.

An untamed expression washed across the face of the golden Dragon. His pupils flared with fire. He inhaled deeply.

Tian Gao's eyes widened. He let go of the blade and leapt out of the way of the jet of flames that ripped through the spot he'd occupied a second before.

Gold flashed out the corner of his eye. Something that felt like a tree trunk with metal barbs slammed into his left thigh. Tian Gao howled, grabbed the Dragon's spiky tail, and ripped it out of his torn flesh.

Something sang through the air by his right ear.

Tian Gao choked on his breath as the Dragon's blade carved his arm from his shoulder. The demon blinked and stared dazedly at his detached limb where it writhed in the grass. Fire lanced through his left elbow in the next instant. Tian Gao looked around in time to see his left forearm thud to the ground, the bleeding vessels cauterized by the sword's flames.

He staggered backward, his pulse pounding in his ears.

Impossible! This is impossible! I'm stronger than this. I cannot possibly be defeat—

Coldness gripped his chest. His gaze dropped to the blade embedded in his heart. Blood gushed up his throat and filled his mouth as the Dragon twisted the sword viciously.

Haruki Kuroda stared into Tian Gao's eyes, his slit-like pupils alight with a golden glow. The light flared. The fire engulfing the sword turned a pure white.

"This is for my brother," the Dragon growled.

The last thing Tian Gao saw was a wall of divine flames.

Hell's power seeped through the widening crack in the middle of the gate and washed across Delacourt's back. He closed his eyes and shivered as the unholy energy amplified that of the demon inside his corrupt soul. A draft kissed his face. He opened his eyes and saw the two angels land lightly before him.

Delacourt smiled. "Welcome, traitors."

Artemus shared a puzzled glance with Drake.

"What the heck do you mean by that?" he asked Delacourt with a frown.

"It is exactly as I say," Delacourt drawled. "You two are traitors who betrayed your brethren thousands of years ago." He touched his chest with a clawed hand. "Who betrayed Asmodee, He who lives inside me."

Drake narrowed his eyes. "I think you have us confused with someone else."

Delacourt laughed raucously. "Trust me, I have the right people." He looked at Artemus. "Your father led the army against us and you bear his blood. Thus, you carry his sin."

"What did you say?" Artemus whispered after a shocked pause.

Delacourt's gaze shifted to Drake. "And you have denounced your lineage. That of our virtuous Second Leader. He Sees The Name." He bared his fangs. "You carry her filthy blood too." He glanced at Artemus. "As do you. I can smell her on both of you."

Artemus took a step forward, his eyes darkening. "Are you talking about our mother? Do you know who she is?!"

A harsh bark of laughter escaped Delacourt. "Oh, I know who that bitch is!" He glared at the scowling angels before him. "But I will not tell you her name! I would rather watch you suffer as you desperately seek to—"

Metal flashed on either side of him.

Delacourt captured the blades curving toward his neck with his bare hands. Shock flared in the angry pairs of blue and crimson-gold eyes before him.

"Oh," Delacourt murmured. "I'm sorry, did that startle you?" He glanced at the dead demons and the piles of ash covering the floor of the chamber behind the two angels, before cocking his head to the side. "Did you think this would be as easy as New York, when you killed Park?"

He cast the angels' blades aside just as two rifts tore open on either side of him. Delacourt grinned, reached inside them, and withdrew two giant broadswords that shimmered with corrupt miasma. He stretched his neck and bowed his back slightly. Black wings tore through his flesh and skin, sprouting from his shoulder blades to frame his body.

Artemus blinked and stared from the dark swords to Delacourt's wings. "Those are new."

CHAPTER THIRTY-NINE

CALLIE PANTED AS SHE RIPPED THE SCEPTER OUT OF THE carcass of the demon hellhound. Smokey released the mangled remains of the second monster some fifteen feet to her right. Crimson gashes covered the hellhound's body where the creature had scored his flesh during their fight.

Callie winced and pressed a hand to the wound in her right flank before limping over to Smokey. "Are you okay, brother?"

Smokey butted his heads gently against her, his eyes flaring with affection.

I am now, sister.

They stared through the gaping hole in the rooftop to the flashes high in the air above them. It was thanks to the divine power coursing through their veins that they could discern the lightning-fast movements of the three figures engaged in a savage battle against the stormy night sky.

Serena and Nate appeared at their side, Elton and the Vatican agents following in their wake. They were all sweating and covered in wounds, Shamus sporting what looked to be a broken left arm.

Serena raised her eyes to the sky. "Who's winning?"

"No one right now," Callie murmured. "Can you see them?"

"Kinda. Or, at least, the nanorobots in my retina can." Serena grimaced. "Besides, all you have to do is listen to figure out where they are."

Violent clangs boomed in the air above them.

The floor shook violently beneath their feet. Callie's heart pounded with fear as she turned toward the gate.

Redness now filled two thirds of the doorway.

"We have to close that! *Now!*"

A rift appeared twenty feet to their left. More demons stepped out of it.

"We've got this," Serena told Callie grimly. "Go take care of the gate!"

Callie and Smokey headed briskly for the head of the room. Haruki appeared on their right, his form now that of a golden dragon.

"Hurry!" Callie glanced at the patch of sky where sparks and bangs arose. "While Artemus and Drake have him distracted!"

Haruki nodded and made for the base of the block of crimson-stained blackness, his expression tense. Corrupt tendrils arced from the doorway and kissed the glittering scales on his skin when he stopped in front of it. He clenched his jaw, grasped his flaming sword in a double-handed grip, and slammed it into the center of the throbbing, red band.

An ungodly noise exploded from the gate. The screams of thousands of demons tore the air asunder.

The black coils entwined around Haruki's arms and legs thickened. His eyes flared with fire. A golden light burst across his scales and burned the foul cords into nothingness.

The doorway started to close.

"*No!*" someone roared.

Callie's eyes widened. She raised the scepter and blocked the broadsword that flashed toward Haruki's back. The floor caved beneath her as she sank half a foot into the ground, her body bowing under the force of the demon wielding the blade. Smokey braced himself against her back to support her, a low continuous growl rumbling out of his throats.

Fury twisted Delacourt's face as he glared at them, his dark wings thumping the air powerfully above their heads. Artemus and Drake flew down, snatched the demon by his arms, and bolted toward the sky.

Two rifts appeared on either side of the closing gate.

Callie and Smokey turned to face the demons materializing out of them.

"I'll take the left," Callie told the hellhound grimly.

Air whooshed out of Artemus's lungs as he swooped beneath a dark blade. He couldn't believe how strong Delacourt was. It was taking both his and Drake's full fighting strength to block the demon's attacks.

Who the heck is this Asmodee guy?!

Blood pearled on a shallow cut on Drake's face. He wiped at it and frowned at the crimson smear on his fingertips.

"Angels can bleed," Delacourt said with a condescending sneer. "They don't often, but they can. Just as demons do."

Drake exchanged a glance with Artemus. "This guy is seriously starting to piss me off."

"I hear you," Artemus muttered, his heart thudding against his ribs.

They attacked, their swords moving as one.

Delacourt's form flickered before vanishing from the spot he'd just occupied. Artemus swore and stopped his blade an inch before it clashed with Drake's. Something slammed into his back and sent him hurtling downward. He smashed through the mansion's rooftop, crashed through the second floor, and ended up inside a study, the ground crumbling beneath the impact of his landing.

Artemus's ears rang as he slowly sat up in the depression in the floor. He ran a thumb across his bloodied lip and scowled.

"Sonofa—" His pulse stuttered. He raised his head and stared at the winged figures visible through the fresh hole in the roof. "No! Drake, stop! Don't do—"

THE DEMON INSIDE DRAKE RAGED AND SCREAMED, HIS will straining against the golden thread that bound him. A red haze descended across Drake's vision as the demon's thirst for battle seeped through him.

He knew he was letting the darkness within him win. But he had no choice. Not against a demon of Delacourt's caliber. He gritted his teeth.

Damnit, I'm gonna have to use his whole strength!

A shout reached Drake's ears. He looked down and saw Artemus take flight, fear darkening his eyes.

"I do not wish to kill you!" Delacourt snarled in front

of him. He swung his broadswords. "But I will if you resist me further, prophecy be damned!"

Drake reached inside his soul and released the devil's shackles.

Darkness filled his world.

CHAPTER FORTY

ARTEMUS'S MOUTH WENT DRY AS A CLOUD OF THROBBING shadows burst around Drake's body. The golden light in the black angel's eyes receded, replaced by pure redness. His face hardened into a deadly mask.

Surprise flashed on Delacourt's face. He hesitated.

A roar erupted from Drake. The black angel moved.

Delacourt gasped.

Artemus froze mid-air, his gaze locked on the black broadsword that had ripped through the giant demon's heart all the way to his back. He hadn't seen the attack and neither had Delacourt.

Drake twisted the blade.

Black blood frothed out of Delacourt's mouth. It dripped down his chin and spilled onto Drake's armor. The demon's eyes fluttered closed. He sagged on the sword that had impaled him, his limp head striking Drake's right shoulder. His body shrank back down to its human form.

Drake grabbed the dead man by the back of his scalp and slowly withdrew the broadsword, an untamed grin twisting his lips.

"No," Artemus mumbled when he discerned his intent. "Drake, stop, he's already—"

A savage sound escaped Drake as he decapitated Delacourt with a single swing of his blade. He watched the man's body drop to the distant ground and cast his mutilated head aside with a dismissive sneer. He turned, his gaze finding the rapidly closing gate and the beast who stood before it. His eyes flashed red. He started to dive.

Artemus moved into the black angel's path.

"Stop," he ordered in a hard voice. "Stop this, *now!*"

Fire lanced through his left forearm. Artemus looked at the sword that had pierced his flesh and scowled.

"That *hurts*, asshole!" he barked, headbutting Drake in the face.

His brother reared back, surprise flickering in his eyes. The redness faded slightly.

Artemus stared into Drake's tortured gaze.

"Help me!" his brother whispered. "I—I don't know how to stop him!"

Artemus swallowed, his heart thumping against his ribs. He did the only thing he could think of.

"We can." He laid a hand on Drake's chest. "Together."

WHITE LIGHT FLARED THROUGH DRAKE'S BODY. He gasped as warmth seeped inside his cold flesh and bones. Awareness slowly returned, the madness in his blood receding. He blinked.

Artemus's face swam before his eyes. "I don't know how much longer I can hold this bastard back, so whatever you have to do, do it *now*, Drake!"

Shock bolted through Drake as he sensed his brother's

power propping the barriers that contained the devil within him. It was enough for him to find the golden thread that had bound the monster and force him inside his prison once more. The devil raged as the walls closed in on him, his voice a dying scream of pure fury.

They both shuddered when Artemus lifted his hand from Drake's chest a moment later.

"Uh-oh," Artemus mumbled, his face turning pale as he examined the hundred-foot drop beneath them.

Air whooshed out of their lips as their bodies and weapons started resuming their original shapes, their powers temporarily depleted by the intense battle with Delacourt.

"Shit," Drake said leadenly, meeting his brother's alarmed stare.

They plunged toward the gaping hole in the rooftop, arms and legs waving wildly.

Smokey broke their fall six feet from the ground.

Artemus grunted when Drake landed on top of him in a tangle of limbs.

"How come I always end up under you?" he groaned.

Drake rolled off him and slid down from Smokey's back. "Probably because I'm the firstborn."

They froze and stared at each other.

"How do I—?" Drake mumbled.

"How do you—?" Artemus started, dropping to the floor.

"Know that?!" they both gasped simultaneously.

Artemus blinked. "I think you're right."

Smokey whined softly, his anxious gaze shifting from Artemus and Drake to the cut on Artemus's left arm.

"I'm okay." Artemus patted the hellhound's flank gently. "See, it's already healing."

Remorse flooded Drake as he stared at the closing wound. "I'm sorry."

"Don't worry about it." Artemus looked toward the gate. It had closed and Haruki was taking the artifact down from the wall. "Well, what do you know? It was a goddamn mirror."

Callie strode toward them ahead of the others, her body human once more. "That was a bit of a wild ride."

Smokey shrank down to his rabbit form and jumped into her arms.

Drake was conscious of the tension underscoring the Chimera's tone. The bonds they shared meant that Callie, Smokey, and Haruki were no doubt aware of what had just happened.

"I know," he said quietly.

Callie stopped in front of Drake and studied him with a thoughtful expression. "Can you control him?"

Drake blinked at the direct question.

He opened his mouth and hesitated. "I want to." He paused. "I *have* to."

Callie squinted at him. He startled when she took his hand in hers.

"You're not alone." She glanced at Smokey and Haruki. "We'll help too."

Haruki nodded, his expression indicating that this was all new to him but he was one of them now.

Serena watched Drake wordlessly, her wary eyes telling him she'd guessed that something serious had just gone down between Artemus and him.

Ogawa appeared in the doorway of the chamber, a group of Vatican agents at his back. The bodyguard's eyes widened.

"What happened?" he mumbled, staring at the disaster zone surrounding them.

"We had an infestation," Artemus said.

Callie wrinkled her nose. "Yeah. Rats. Big ones."

Haruki grimaced. "Pest control was a bitch."

CHAPTER FORTY-ONE

"Thank you for your business," Otis said with a smile.

The couple nodded and headed for the exit, their eyes glowing with excitement at having found the wedding rings of their dreams. The door closed after them with a jingle.

Otis's smile disappeared. He glanced at the fading light outside the antique shop and walked out from behind the counter to put the "Closed" sign up. He studied the street outside through the glass partition in the front door before turning on his heels and heading for the back of the building.

Five days had passed since he'd last seen Artemus. His boss had called him in a rush late one morning to say he was going to L.A. on Vatican business and might be gone a while.

Otis knew that was code for demons.

A heavy feeling settled over him as he climbed the stairs to his apartment. The debate that had raged inside him day and night for the last few weeks reared its ugly head once more.

It wasn't that he was being a coward for not engaging with Artemus and his new friends, or for refusing to get involved with Ba'al and anything to do with demons. It was true that the idea such creatures existed horrified him and that the account his father had related to them about the circumstances surrounding Otis's mother's confinement to a psychiatric hospital and her eventual death haunted him still.

If he were to choose one word to describe his feelings, then it was torn. He was torn between his desire to distance himself from the things that had led to his mother's tragic spiral into what everyone had thought was madness at the time and his longing to help Artemus and his friends prepare for the upcoming war.

Otis clenched his jaw and entered his dark living room.

Because a war is coming. This I'm certain of.

He flicked the light switch on and gazed grimly at the journals and reference books strewn across the room.

ARTEMUS STRODE BRISKLY ALONG THE SIDEWALK.

"By the way, why are we walking?" Callie asked.

He glanced at her and the rabbit hopping by her feet. "It's a nice evening. I thought the fresh air would do us all some good."

"The fresh air is cold, is what it is," Haruki muttered. He shivered and burrowed his hands inside the pockets of his leather jacket.

Drake studied Artemus thoughtfully. "You know, there's something I've been meaning to ask you."

"What?" Artemus said.

"Why don't you have a ride?"

Silence fell across their group as they entered the outskirts of Old Town.

"He's right," Callie murmured. "You don't have a car."

Drake cocked an eyebrow. "What, are you a bad driver or something?"

Artemus remained resolutely mute.

Suspicion darkened his brother's face. "You *do* have a driver's license, right?"

Artemus frowned.

Callie gasped. Haruki's eyes widened.

"Jesus," Drake snorted, "who the hell doesn't have a driver's license in this day and age? I mean, the cars practically drive themselves!"

"I did have one," Artemus mumbled. "It was revoked." He hesitated. "Because of the accidents."

"*Accidents?*" Drake grimaced. "As in plural?"

Artemus sniffed. "Cars are the tools of the devil."

A mocking smile curved Drake's mouth. "Nah, you're just a shit driver."

Artemus scowled. They came in sight of the antique shop. He entered the building and made for the stairs ahead of the others.

"Hey, Otis, I'm back." He knocked briskly on Otis's apartment door before opening it. "There's something I hope you can—"

Artemus froze two steps inside the brightly-lit lounge.

Otis sat on the couch opposite the entrance, a spoonful of steaming soup halfway to his mouth and some dozen journals scattered on the low table in front of him. More crowded the floor, alongside several textbooks and loose stacks of paper.

Artemus stared at the mess. "What the heck is going on here?"

Some soup tumbled out of the spoon and splashed onto a startled Otis's lap. "Shit!"

His assistant grabbed a napkin and dabbed furiously at his pants.

～

"OTIS, THIS IS HARUKI KURODA," ARTEMUS SAID. "Haruki, Otis Boone."

Haruki studied the pale young man with the glasses who sat twisting his hands nervously on the couch opposite him.

Otis Boone wasn't quite what he'd been expecting when Artemus had told him about what had gone down in Pittsburgh a few weeks ago. For one thing, Haruki couldn't feel anything from him. Just as Artemus had explained, Otis did not project any energy that hinted at hidden abilities or a connection with the rest of them.

"Why are you here?" Otis mumbled, his gaze not quite meeting Artemus's.

"This *is* my shop." Artemus frowned. "More to the point, what is all this?"

He indicated the journals and papers littering the floor and the table.

Otis remained tight-lipped.

Artemus sighed. "These look like copies of your mother's journals."

"They are," Otis finally muttered.

Artemus grimaced and rubbed the back of his neck. "Does this mean you've decided to help us after all?"

Otis's eyes darkened. His hands fisted on his lap. "I don't really have a choice in the matter now, do I?!"

The room trembled. Glass rattled in the windows. The bowl of soup on the coffee table danced across the wooden surface.

Haruki's eyes widened.

Otis scowled at the porcelain dish containing his dinner as if it had committed a deadly sin. "Damn it!"

Artemus stared at his assistant. "Is it getting stronger?"

Haruki glanced between the two of them with a frown. He didn't know what it was that had caused the phenomenon they'd just witnessed but he knew it had originated from the angry young man glaring at Artemus.

"Yes!" Otis snapped. "And I've been having dreams too!"

CHAPTER FORTY-TWO

"They started after we came back from Pittsburgh."

Drake studied Otis where he sat next to Artemus.

"And what is it you're dreaming of, exactly?" Callie asked quietly.

Otis propped his elbows on his knees and rubbed his temples.

"The past, I think," he muttered. "And possibly the future."

Drake exchanged a surprised glance with Artemus.

"I keep seeing flashes of this battle," Otis continued in a troubled voice. "It wasn't in this world, that I'm certain of."

"Was it the War in Heaven?" Artemus asked after a pause. "The one your father and Elton told us about?"

Otis hesitated before dipping his chin. "Yes, probably." He paused. "And I was part of it."

Smokey's ears twitched where he perched on Callie's lap.

Callie sucked in a breath. "What?"

"I was in that battle," Otis said stiffly. "As in, a fully participating member of the divine army, with golden armor and a sword and everything." A humorless chuckle escaped him. "Can you imagine it? Me, an *angel?!*"

"Why not?"

Otis blinked and stared at Artemus.

Drake's brother glanced around the room. "What makes you less worthy than any of us?"

Otis swallowed convulsively, his eyes uneasy.

"Look, none of us asked for this," Artemus continued quietly. "None of us *wished* to become the things that we are. But this, whatever *this* is, is beyond our control." His expression hardened. "Everything that has happened to us was preordained, to a certain extent. And I'm convinced there are forces at work behind the scenes that we are not yet aware of. Our only chance to survive what is coming is to stick together and try to unravel this mystery."

"You said you dreamt about the future," Callie said in the silence that befell them. "Did you see—" She hesitated. "Did you see how it all ends?"

Otis frowned. "I'm not sure. It's all so hazy and disjointed."

"You didn't happen to, er, spot a woman with brown hair and blue eyes in those dreams of yours, did you?" Artemus asked suddenly.

Drake blinked at the urgency in his brother's voice.

"You mean, Serena Blake?" Otis said.

"No. This woman's hair is a richer brown, like chocolate.' Artemus hesitated. "And her eyes are a deeper blue, like the sea when the sun strikes it."

Otis shook his head. "I don't think so."

"What, she your secret squeeze?" Haruki asked in a teasing tone.

The tips of Artemus's ears turned red. "Not telling."

Haruki's jaw dropped open.

Callie gasped and brought her hands to her mouth. "Oh my God, she is, isn't she? You're having sex dreams about this girl, aren't you?!"

Smokey's eyes rounded.

"I'm *not* having sex dreams about her!" Artemus protested between gritted teeth, his cheeks darkening with color.

Haruki grinned. "Yeah, you are, you horndog."

Artemus scowled. He pointed a finger at Smokey. "And you, stop looking at me as if I'm a pervert!"

The rabbit huffed.

Drake narrowed his eyes at his brother, not quite sure why he felt so disgruntled at the fact he didn't know anything about this.

"So, who's this chick?" he grumbled.

Something that looked like guilt flashed on Artemus's face. "She's—" He stopped and ran a hand through his hair. "She's someone I've been dreaming of all my life." A cynical half-smile curved his lips. "I mean, after it turned into a shit show in 2017."

"And you've never met her?" Callie asked, her face filling with wonder.

His brother's eyes turned sad for an instant. "No."

"By the way, what happened in L.A.?" Otis asked curiously.

Artemus's expression cleared. "Oh, yeah. That's why we're here. We found another one."

"Found another what?" Otis said.

"Show him," Artemus told Haruki.

Haruki hesitated before rising to his feet. He unleashed the blade inside his bracelet.

"Flaming Sword of Camael," Otis said immediately.

Haruki blinked, his shocked gaze moving from Otis to the sword and back.

"Wow," he murmured. "Artemus was right. And here I thought you were just a dweeb."

Artemus raised an eyebrow. "Alright, who's this Camael guy?"

"He was the Archangel of Strength, Courage, and War," Drake said before Otis could reply. "He was apparently the one who drove Adam and Eve out of the Garden of Eden." He pulled a face at Artemus's surprised stare. "Have you not been doing *any* research on the stuff Otis's father told us about?"

"No," Artemus replied bluntly.

Drake sighed.

"You're correct," Otis said. "Camael was also known as the One Who Stands Before God. Although he's not formally recognized by the Catholic Church as an Archangel, like the seven other highest Seraphims, many believe he was as powerful as them." He studied Haruki with widening eyes. "Does that mean you are—?"

"No," Artemus interrupted. "The sword may be his, but Haruki isn't an angel. He's the Colchian Dragon."

Otis paled.

Lines furrowed Haruki's brow. "I don't think these weapons are ours."

They stared at him.

"What do you mean?" Drake asked.

"I sensed it when we were in L.A., back at that movie producer's place in Hollywood Hills." The sword transformed back into a bracelet. Haruki touched the beads lightly. "That my weapon was not mine. That I had been granted the right to use it, albeit temporarily, by its true owner." He looked at them, his expression growing confident. "My beast was in agreement."

"I think you're right," Otis mumbled after a short silence. "I don't know how I know this, I just...do, I guess."

"The battle in L.A. was on a different level to the one we fought in New York." Artemus glanced uneasily at Drake. "The demon commander Drake and I clashed with was incredibly powerful. He said his demon was called Asmodee."

Otis drew a sharp breath. "Asmodee?"

"Yeah, that's the name he told us," Drake muttered.

The events of that day still haunted his thoughts. Even though Artemus had helped him confine the devil within, the fact that Drake had reveled in that incredible power and thirsted for more in those scant minutes the demon had had full control of his body worried him. He wasn't sure they would be able to put the monster back in his box again if he were to escape in the future.

"Asmodee is reputed to be a Prince of Hell," Otis said.

Callie frowned. "A prince?"

"Well, a lower prince," Otis said. "Michael Psellus was an 11th century Greek monk who wrote a treatise entitled the Classification of Demons. The demonic hierarchy he described therein closely mimics that of Heaven. But it was in The Book of Abramelin, penned by an Egyptian magician from the 15th century, that a subclassification of the highest ranking of Hell was first described. Abramelin spoke of four Princes of Hell: Satan, Belial, Lucifer, and Leviathan. And beneath them were eight sub-princes: Amaymon, Ariton, Astaroth, Maggot, Beelzebub, Oriens, Paimon, and Asmodee."

Callie shivered. "Jeez, their names alone give me the heebie-jeebies."

Artemus stared at Drake. "Does this mean you killed a Prince of Hell?"

"I didn't particularly have a choice in the matter, remember?" Drake retorted.

The devil inside him had stirred slightly when Otis had uttered the names of the twelve demonic princes. Drake frowned.

Which means he's probably right.

A pained expression dawned on Artemus's face. "There's something else. The demon also told us our fathers' names, in an indirect fashion."

Callie straightened in her seat. "What?!" She looked accusingly from Artemus to Drake. "You never said anything about this when we were in L.A.!"

"Yeah, well, I wanted to discuss it with Otis first," Artemus mumbled. He looked at his assistant. "He said my father led the army against the demons." He paused. "And that Drake's father was their Second Leader."

"He Sees The Name," Drake added.

What little color was left drained from Otis's face.

He swallowed and turned to Artemus. "Considering the sword you possess, that would make you the son of the Archangel Michael." He looked at Drake, his eyes dark with worry. "The Second Leader of the Grigori was a powerful Fallen Angel called Samyaza. His other designation was—He Sees The Name."

Shocked silence descended around them.

Haruki scratched his cheek. "So, angels can have sex?"

Artemus's mouth fell open.

"Really?!" he spluttered. "That's what you just took from that?"

Haruki shrugged. "It kinda feels icky."

"One of the reasons the Fallen Angels were cast into Hell was precisely because they slept with human women," Otis explained. "And they were said to have borne children with them too. The giant Nephilims."

Haruki pulled a face. "I don't think I want to meet one of those."

Artemus sighed and turned to Otis. "Anyway, what's going on here?" He indicated the journals and books on the floor. "Are you trying to translate your mother's writings?"

Otis hesitated before nodding. "Yes. But I haven't gotten very far. And neither will the Vatican, if my suspicions are correct."

Drake stared. "What do you mean?"

Otis took his glasses off and rubbed a hand down his face.

"Because my mother wrote a code within a code. And I don't think anyone we know can break it."

Artemus arched an eyebrow. "We'll just have to find someone who can, then, won't we?"

CHAPTER FORTY-THREE

LIGHT DANCED ACROSS ARTEMUS'S EYELIDS. HE groaned, turned over, and burrowed his face in the pillow. The bedroom door squeaked open. He opened one eye and saw Smokey hop out of the room.

The antique clock on the nightstand caught his gaze.

"For God's sake, who the hell wakes up at seven on a freaking Sunday?!" Artemus mumbled.

The next time he opened his eyes, it was ten. He rolled onto his back, stretched his arms above his head, and yawned. He was surprised the others hadn't woken him up. Although the mansion was huge, his new tenants had an annoying habit of making a lot of noise, especially first thing in the morning.

Two weeks had passed since their trip to L.A. Things were finally returning to normal in Chicago and spring had started to give way to summer. Bar the fact that they were still embroiled in some mysterious plan involving the Apocalypse, Artemus would go as far as to say that life was good.

His light mood faded. A faint frown wrinkled his brow.

The battle in L.A. had proven one thing. They could not afford to be blasé about Ba'al. New York had given them a false sense of confidence. Though they were all powerful in their own right, they had gotten their asses kicked pretty badly before averting an all-out disaster in L.A.

With the second gate now in the possession of the Vatican, Artemus hoped they would soon find answers to the questions they had about their origins and their roles in the war still to come.

It was after the fight in Malibu that Artemus had learned that the antique shop in Santa Ana where the mirror had ended up had an iron vault in its basement. That, combined with the fact that the strongbox it had been stored in was also made of iron, explained why both the demons in L.A. and Haruki had been unable to sense it from afar.

The reasons as to why Yashiro Kuroda had split up the antiques he'd collected from the hotel and sent them all over the county would remain an enigma. Artemus couldn't help but suspect that someone not of this world had had a hand in it, somehow.

Also troubling was the conversation Artemus had had with Elton a week ago, when they'd caught up at the auction house. His mentor had been busy writing a report for the Vatican about the events in L.A. One thing had become clear when Elton and Isaac had gone over what had happened. The fact that Delacourt had seemed to know all about their trip to L.A. and their whereabouts in the city could only mean one thing.

There was a mole in the Vatican leaking information to Ba'al about the group's investigations.

Security at the secret location where Callie and Haruki's gates were being kept had doubled since and an internal investigation had been arranged by the Pope herself to look into the matter.

A noise outside distracted Artemus from his dark thoughts.

He pushed the covers off his legs, padded over to the tall, leaded windows, and yanked the curtains open. "What the—?"

Artemus grabbed a T-shirt from an armchair, shrugged it over his head, and left the bedroom at a brisk pace. Muted voices reached him when he neared the main staircase. He started down the steps and froze on the split-level landing.

A stack of boxes and several suitcases sat in the middle of the grand foyer. They were being guarded by four Asian men in suits. The guards stiffened when they saw him. They bowed respectfully.

"Steele-sama," they said in a chorus.

"Seriously, what the hell is going on here?" Artemus muttered.

He descended the rest of the stairs and spotted Serena, Drake, Nate, Callie, and Smokey in the doorway of the TV room. "Hey, guys, why are there, like, a dozen cars parked on the—?"

Artemus froze when he looked past them.

The TV room was filled with Asian men in suits. The furniture had been cleared to the edges of the floor and they were all kneeling rigidly on thin pillows in an orderly formation of rows.

At the head of the group, behind a low table bearing a traditional Japanese ceramic cup, was Akihito Kuroda. An embarrassed-looking Haruki sat slightly behind and to his father's right, while Ogawa knelt in a similar position to the left of the Kuroda Group leader.

Akihito Kuroda's face brightened when he saw Artemus. "Ah. Mr. Steele. So good of you to finally join us."

"I am *so* sorry," Haruki mouthed silently behind his father.

Unease filtered through Artemus when he spotted what looked like some kind of shrine next to the fireplace.

Serena turned and placed a heavy hand on his shoulder.

"Congratulations," the super soldier said solemnly. "I believe you just bagged yourself a rich Japanese bride."

Callie giggled. Drake smiled.

"Hey!" Haruki protested, rising on one knee. "I told you guys this isn't like that!"

Akihito Kuroda cut his eyes to his son.

Haruki dropped back down to the floor. "Sorry, father."

Akihito Kuroda indicated the thin pillow opposite him. "Mr. Steele, would you care to join us?"

Artemus frowned. "What is this about?"

Two guards rose from the floor, walked over to him, took his arms, and gently guided him to kneel on the pillow.

"Okaaay." Artemus folded his arms across his chest while the men returned to their seats. "I'm sitting. Now, talk."

Akihito Kuroda smiled. "Why don't you have a drink first?"

Artemus looked at the straw-colored liquid in the cup. He shrugged. "Alright, but jasmine tea isn't really my thing."

He reached for the cup. Haruki's eyes widened.

"Er, Artemus—" Serena started behind him as he brought the cup to his lips.

"I wouldn't do that if I were—" Drake warned.

Artemus downed the drink and froze.

"Oh, boy," Nate muttered.

Artemus grimaced, wiped his mouth with the back of his hand, and put the cup down.

He glared accusingly at Haruki's father. "That was *not* jasmine tea!"

"You dumbass!" Drake snapped.

Artemus scowled at his brother. "What?"

Akihito Kuroda beamed. "Welcome to the family."

Artemus blinked. "Huh?"

Haruki put a hand over his eyes and muttered something rude under his breath.

"You just exchanged a sake cup with the head of a Yakuza group," Serena said sharply. "Which means you just got accepted into the Japanese mafia brotherhood, you moron!"

"No, it doesn't," Artemus denied.

"Do you *not* watch martial arts movies?" Drake barked.

"No," Artemus replied bluntly. He turned to Haruki's father. "They're kidding, right? I didn't just become, I don't know, something stupid like—like a *Yakuza*, right?"

The Kuroda Group members stiffened. Palpable tension filled the TV room.

"I take back 'stupid,'" Artemus mumbled with a sickly smile.

"I assure you, we treat our rituals with deadly seriousness, Mr. Steele," Akihito Kuroda said stiffly.

Artemus swallowed hard. "Deadly, huh?"

Akihito Kuroda's face relaxed.

"You are now officially a member of the Kuroda Group," the older man explained in a gentle voice. "You will receive the assistance of our syndicate wherever you go in the world. Which means I can safely leave Haruki in your care. He needs to be with you."

Artemus stared. "Huh?"

"Yeah, so, about that." A sheepish expression dawned on Haruki's face. "I'm, er, moving in." He cocked a thumb at his father. "I told the old man I had to be with you guys and he was like," Haruki deepened his voice to imitate his father's somber timbre, "'*We need to make things official,*' and shit, so, here we are."

A weak chuckle left the Yakuza heir's lips. It died in the face of Artemus's expression and his father's frown.

"*Whaaaat?!*" Artemus screeched.

Ogawa kowtowed to Artemus. The rest of the guards followed.

"I hope you will take care of our young master," the bodyguard said somberly. "He will be sorely missed."

"Well, you can have him back!" Artemus snarled.

Akihito Kuroda narrowed his eyes. "You destroyed my mansion. I think you owe me something in return."

Artemus leaned toward the Kuroda Group head.

"First of all, your kid there," he hissed, indicating Haruki with a cocked thumb, "started that damn fire! Secondly, we saved your butts from some pretty nasty demons!"

"Irrespective of that, Haruki is now bound to you," Akihito Kuroda countered smoothly.

Haruki blew out an exasperated sigh.

"I'm telling you, father, we don't have that kind of relationship! Besides," he pointed an accusing finger at Artemus, "this guy has some—some *chick* he keeps having hentai dreams about!"

"Oh." Ogawa stared at Artemus. "And he looks so innocent too."

Surprised mutters rose from the other guards.

"You're allowed one mistress," Akihito Kuroda stated magnanimously.

A muffled snort sounded from the doorway.

Artemus glared at Callie where she was leaning against Serena, tears of laughter dancing in her eyes. The super soldier was grinning.

"Maybe we should have red rice for dinner tonight," Nate murmured.

"Oh yeah." Serena's grin widened. "That's what they have at Japanese weddings, right?"

A choked sound escaped Drake.

"I—" he swallowed and cleared his throat, "I can't!"

Artemus's brother turned and headed into the foyer, shoulders shaking.

"That's it!" Artemus jumped to his feet. "I'm going to have a shower! When I'm done, you all," he jabbed a finger at the Kuroda Group members, "better be gone from this place!"

He stormed out of the room.

"But I made breakfast for everyone," Nate protested.

"Like I give a rat's ass!" Artemus roared over his shoulder. He stopped and glared at Haruki. "And where the hell are you going?"

Haruki blinked innocently. "To check out my room."

"You have no room!"

Haruki rolled his eyes. "Oh, come on! It makes sense to stick together." He waved his arms. "You said so yourself! So how about you give me—"

A loud crash echoed around the vestibule.

"—a break?" Haruki finished weakly.

They all stared at the smashed pieces of the porcelain antique he'd knocked off a console table.

"Was that a Qing Dynasty vase?" Akihito Kuroda murmured, peering around Ogawa's shoulder.

"I believe it was, boss," the bodyguard mumbled.

Haruki paled. His gaze shifted to Artemus. "Look, man, it was an accident, okay?"

"Unleash your sword," Artemus ordered between gritted teeth.

Haruki blinked. "Huh?"

"I said, unleash your sword, Haruki!" Artemus growled.

"Uh-oh," Nate said. "I think he's gonna blow."

"You're right." Serena stared at Artemus's left temple. "That vein is back."

Smokey jumped into Callie's arms and buried his face in her chest.

"Hey, now," Drake started, hands raised in a pacifying gesture as he crossed the foyer toward Artemus, "I'm sure the vase can be fixed, so why don't you calm—"

White light exploded across the vestibule. Artemus hefted his flaming broadsword over his shoulder, his wings beating the air with steady thumps as he glared at them from mid-air.

"Oh shit," Haruki said leadenly.

THE END

∾

AFTERWORD

Thank you for reading FIRE AND EARTH! The next book in LEGION is AWAKENING.

If you enjoyed FIRE AND EARTH, please consider leaving a review on your favorite book site. Reviews help readers find books! Join my VIP Facebook Group for exclusive sneak peeks at my upcoming books and sign up to my newsletter for new release alerts, exclusive bonus content, and giveaways.

Turn the page to read an extract from AWAKENING now!

AWAKENING EXTRACT

1857, ENGLAND

It was the scream that woke him. The boy bolted upright in the four-poster bed, the sheets crumpling to his waist. He blinked before looking dazedly around his bedroom, the remains of his nightmare fading to wisps of darkness in the night. Moonlight washed through the leaded windows of the Victorian mansion in bright beams, illuminating the empty chamber around him.

For one wild moment, the boy wondered if the sound had been part of the terrible dream he'd been having. The same dream he'd experienced every night for the past month. The one where monsters dwelled.

The scream came again. This time, it spoke of unspeakable pain and terror.

A whimper left the boy's lips when he recognized his mother's tortured voice.

There was no longer any doubt in his mind. This, whatever was transpiring on this cold winter's night, was no dream.

Another voice joined his mother's desperate cries.

The boy's eyes widened as his father's horrified yells echoed down the west wing hallway.

He scrambled out of bed and stood frozen for a moment, the cold floorboards beneath his feet sapping away what little warmth remained in his body. His gaze found the poker by the fireplace.

The dying embers in the hearth painted a macabre red glow across the metal.

The boy walked over on trembling legs and closed his hand around the handle, his pulse racing with fear. More voices reached him.

His sisters were sobbing and begging, their tones rising with every desperate word they uttered, their panic so thick it paralyzed him once more. They stopped abruptly, their pleas cut off by a grisly, fleshy sound.

Deathly silence fell upon the mansion. The boy waited, mouth dry and heart pounding so fast he feared it would leap from his chest.

The noise that came next caused his bladder to loosen. Warm wetness pooled between his legs as an inhuman shriek tore through his home.

It was the same sound he'd heard the monsters in his nightmares make.

A heavy footfall made the floor tremble. Something was coming down the hallway toward his room. Something big. Something that scratched the wood with every wicked step.

A vile stench tickled the boy's nostrils.

A shadow appeared across the gap beneath his bedroom door. The floorboards dipped slightly as the monster stopped outside.

The boy took a step back. A gasp whooshed out of him

as he slipped on his own urine and landed heavily on his backside.

A scraping noise danced across the outside of the door, the sound setting the boy's teeth on edge even as he scrambled desperately to his feet.

"*Fie, foh, and fum,*" the monster growled, "*I smell the blood of an Englishman.*"

Tears overflowed the boy's eyes and ran down his icy cheeks. He swallowed the sobs rising in his chest.

His family was dead. He knew this without question.

And the monster who had murdered them, the one from his darkest nightmares, the one now standing outside his room, was going to kill him too. Terror and despair swamped him, a heavy mantle that weighed his small body down. His shoulders sagged. His fingers loosened around the poker.

There was no point fighting his fate.

Thump.

The boy blinked, the monster temporarily forgotten. Before he could fathom the eerie throbbing he'd just sensed inside the very marrow of his soul, the bedroom door exploded inward in a cloud of deadly shards and splinters. A cry left him, unbidden.

The monster appeared through the falling debris, reeking of death and rotting flesh. It was over six feet tall, with a hulking physique, its hands and feet tipped by wicked, blood-soaked talons. Its eyes were black but for their yellow centers.

The boy registered the gore and gristle coating the monster's lower face and realized he was looking at what remained of his parents and sisters. Rage erupted inside of him then, so sudden and so fierce he almost gasped with the force of it.

Thump-thump.

There was no time to explore the heavy beat that was matching his own frantic heart or the uncanny warmth rising from the depths of his body. The boy widened his stance and gripped the poker in white-knuckled fists, the fury he was experiencing echoed by something inside him. Something that he knew instinctively was not of this world.

Gone was the crippling fear that had gripped him a moment past. In its place was deadly determination.

Thump-thump. Thump-thump.

Heat bloomed on the boy's right palm. Though he caught a faint glow between his fingers out the corner of his eye, he did not dare look away from the monster who had just stepped inside his room.

To do so would be to invite instant death.

The boy and the monster stared at one another for a frozen moment in time. In the monster's obsidian eyes, the boy detected surprise and a hint of interest. The monster smiled, its features twisting in a ghastly grimace of loathing and hunger. It rushed toward the boy, its movements so swift he almost missed its charge.

White light filled the room.

Get Awakening now!

ABOUT A.D. STARRLING

Want to know about AD Starrling's upcoming releases?
Sign up to her newsletter for new release alerts, sneak
peeks, giveaways, and get a free boxset and exclusive
freebies.

Join AD's reader group on Facebook:
The Seventeen Club

Like AD's Author Page

Check out AD's website for extras and more:
www.adstarrling.com

BOOKS BY A.D. STARRLING

SEVENTEEN NOVELS

Hunted - 1

Warrior - 2

Empire - 3

Legacy - 4

Origins - 5

Destiny - 6

SEVENTEEN NOVEL BOXSETS

The Seventeen Collection 1 - Books 1-3

The Seventeen Collection 2 - Books 4-6

SEVENTEEN SHORT STORIES

First Death - 1

Dancing Blades - 2

The Meeting - 3

The Warrior Monk - 4

LEGION

DIVISION EIGHT

MISCELLANEOUS

Void - A Sci-fi Horror Short Story

The Other Side of the Wall - A Horror Short Story

AUDIOBOOKS

Go to Authors Direct for a range of options where you can get AD's audiobooks.